Terror on Every Side!
THE LIFE OF JEREMIAH

VOLUME 1 – Early Days

Mark Morgan

Second Edition with extra resources, 2020
ISBN (eBook): 978-1-925587-15-9
➢ ISBN (Paperback 9.5pt): 978-1-925587-09
ISBN (Paperback 10.5pt): 978-1-925587-17

Bible Tales

www.BibleTales.online

Cover picture: Jerusalem from the Mount of Olives
by Frederick Edwin Church (1870).

Free Download

Paul in Snippets

A 109-page PDF novelette by Mark Morgan.

The life of Paul painted from the Acts of the Apostles.

Get your free copy of *Paul in Snippets* when you sign up for the Bible Tales mailing list. As well as the eBook, you will receive a weekly email newsletter with micro tales, informative articles and special offers.

Visit **https://www.BibleTales.online/free-pins**

www.BibleTales.online

To my ever-patient wife, Ruth.

Acknowledgements and thanks

The story contained in this book was started because of my daughter, Heidi, who, on being prompted by me to write a Bible-based story, said that I should show her how! It was written over two years with each chapter being sent to a group initially made up of close family members and later extended to a slightly wider audience.

Particular thanks are due to Ruth, my wife, who let me take the time to write, patiently read what I wrote, and humoured me when I spent inordinate amounts of time on research into minute details.

Feedback from early readers and subscribers has improved the story greatly, so I thank them. No manuscript is ever without errors, but these early readers helped eliminate most typos, bad grammar and uncomfortable usage, particularly my befuddled use of tenses. The greatest thanks in this area go to the one who did the most work: Cathy, my oldest daughter, who has tirelessly undertaken the thankless task of proof reading the entire manuscript more than once.

My son Chris has helped with various technical details, including the Bible Tales logo, and his excellent reading has made the audiobook a pleasure to listen to.

The map on page 12 of the Babylonian Empire in about 600BC was derived from a map of the Middle East[1] by Yiyi[2] with a CC BY 3.0 licence.[3] The "derivative work" in this book is released under the same CC BY 3.0 licence.

---

[1] https://commons.wikimedia.org/wiki/File:Near_East_ topographic_map_with_toponyms_3000bc-pt.svg

[2] https://commons.wikimedia.org/wiki/User:Yiyi

[3] https://creativecommons.org/licenses/by/3.0/deed.en

The map of Israel and Judah on page 13 was based on a public domain SVG map of Israel and its borders from 1949 to 1967[4] and is also released into the public domain.

The map of Jerusalem on page 14 started with a public domain map of Jerusalem[5] heavily edited based on a large number of other sources. The contours were added using NASA data through Maperative[6]. Other sources include Army Map Service 1961, Series K931, Sheet Jerusalem 2, Edition 2-AMS.[7]

A request

I have a request to make of all you readers. If you find any errors; typos, spelling errors, poor grammar, unkempt use of vocabulary, or, most importantly, errors of fact where the story misrepresents the Bible, please let me know. I can't correct printed books, but electronic versions and new printed editions can be fixed.

---

[4] https://commons.wikimedia.org/wiki/File:Israel_1949-1967.svg

[5] https://commons.wikimedia.org/wiki/File:C%2BB-Jerusalem-Map2-WallsAndContours.svg

[6] http://maperitive.net/

[7] https://legacy.lib.utexas.edu/maps/world_cities/txu-oclc-36445576-jerusalem-1961.jpg

VOLUME ONE
Early Days

Contents

"Terror on Every Side!"

For I hear the whispering of many—
terror on every side!—
as they scheme together against me,
as they plot to take my life.

A psalm of David: Psalm 31:13

For I hear many whispering.
Terror is on every side!
"Denounce him! Let us denounce him!"
say all my close friends,
watching for my fall.
"Perhaps he will be deceived;
then we can overcome him
and take our revenge on him."

Jeremiah 20:10

Jeremiah's family tree

The book of Jeremiah begins by telling us that he was a priest, the son of Hilkiah.   Hilkiah was the High Priest.

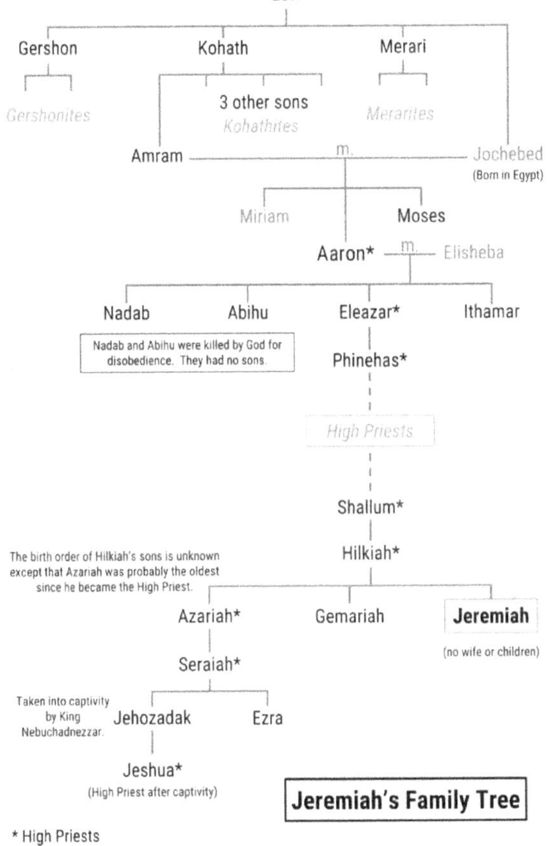

* High Priests

Gedaliah's family tree

Shaphan was the Secretary who read the Book of the Law to King Josiah. His sons and grandsons also filled important places in the life of Jeremiah.

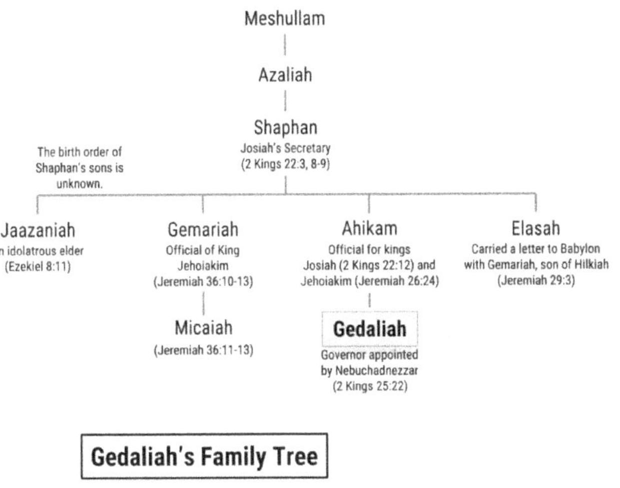

Maps

In the first chapter of the book of Jeremiah, he was told that he had been chosen to be a prophet to the nations.   He was given messages for many different nations. Most of the nations that are furthest away from his home in Judah are shown in the map below.   The locations that were closer to his home in Anathoth are shown in the maps on the following pages.

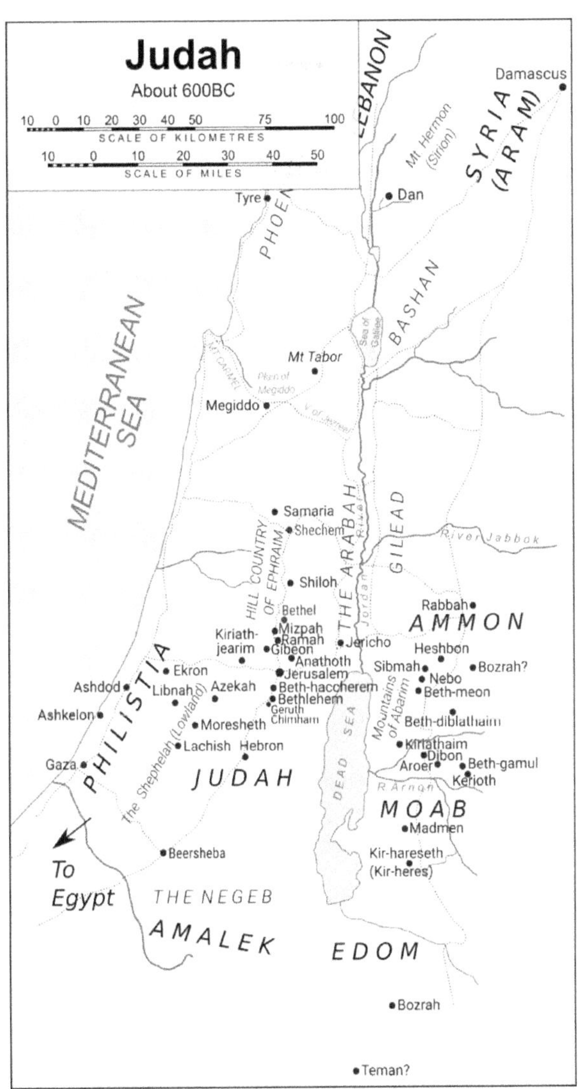

Judah
About 600BC
10 0 10 20 30 40 50 75 100
SCALE OF KILOMETRES
10 0 10 20 30 40 50
SCALE OF MILES
LEBANON
Damascus
SYRIA (ARAM)
Mt Hermon (Sirion)
Dan
PHOEN
Tyre
BASHAN
MEDITERRANEAN SEA
Mt Carmel
Sea of Galilee
Mt Tabor
Plain of Megiddo
V of Jezreel
Megiddo
THE ARABAH
Jordan River
GILEAD
River Jabbok
Samaria
Shechem
HILL COUNTRY OF EPHRAIM
Shiloh
Bethel
Rabbah
AMMON
Mizpah
Ramah
Kiriath-jearim
Gibeon
Jericho
Heshbon
Anathoth
Jerusalem
Sibmah
Bozrah?
Ekron
Nebo
Azekah
Beth-haccherem
Beth-meon
Ashdod
Libnah
Bethlehem
Mountains of Abarim
Ashkelon
Geruth Chimham
Beth-diblathaim
Moresheth
DEAD SEA
Kiriathaim
Lachish
Hebron
Aroer
Dibon
Beth-gamul
Gaza
PHILISTIA
Kerioth
The Shephelah (Lowland)
JUDAH
R Arnon
MOAB
Madmen
To Egypt
Beersheba
Kir-hareseth (Kir-heres)
THE NEGEB
AMALEK
EDOM
Bozrah
Teman?

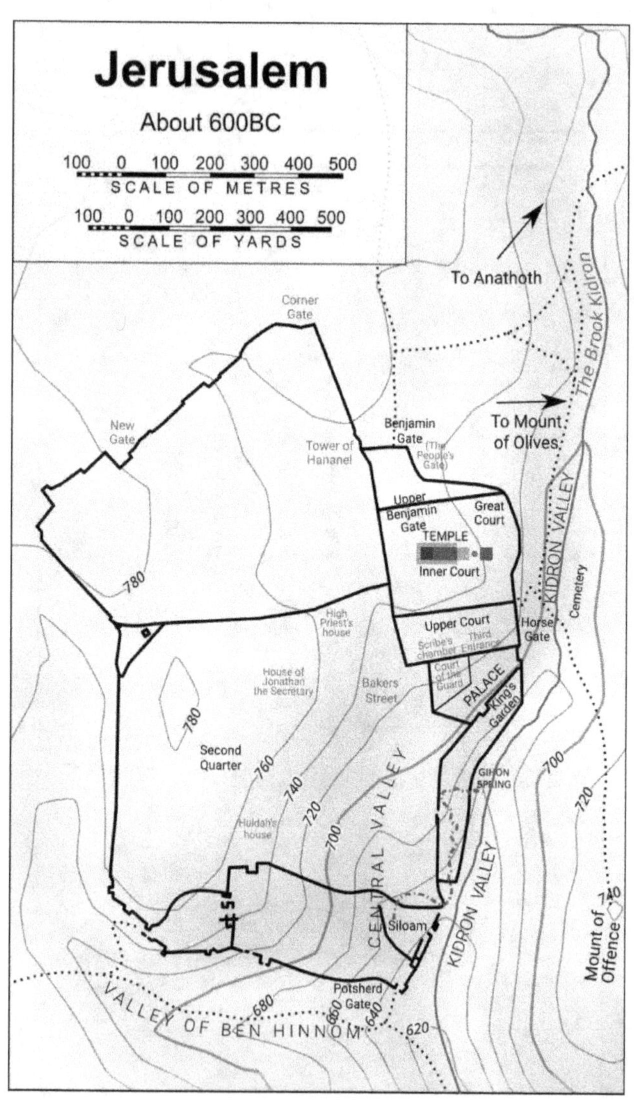

Jerusalem
About 600BC
100 0 100 200 300 400 500
SCALE OF METRES
100 0 100 200 300 400 500
SCALE OF YARDS
To Anathoth
The Brook Kidron
Corner Gate
New Gate
Benjamin Gate
(The People's Gate)
Tower of Hananel
To Mount of Olives
Upper Benjamin Gate
Great Court
TEMPLE
Inner Court
KIDRON VALLEY
Cemetery
780
High Priest's house
Upper Court
Scribe's chamber
Third Entrance
Horse Gate
House of Jonathan the Secretary
Bakers Street
Court of the Guard
PALACE
King's Garden
780
Second Quarter
760
740
720
700
GIHON SPRING
700
720
Huldah's house
700
CENTRAL VALLEY
KIDRON VALLEY
Mount of Offence
740
Siloam
Potsherd Gate
680
660
640
620
VALLEY OF BEN HINNOM

Timeline

We do not know how old Jeremiah was when he began to prophesy, all we know is that it was in the 13th year of King Josiah. All the ages on this timeline assume that Jeremiah was then 17 years old. If we assume a different age, all of the ages given must be adjusted likewise.

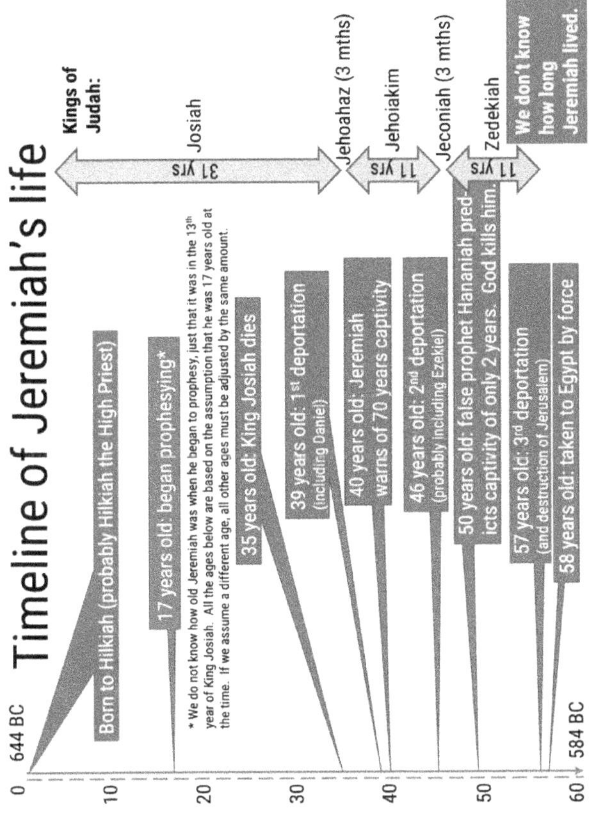

Chapter 1

My Birthday

March, 585BC

It was on my seventeenth birthday that I first heard – or felt – God's voice. In those days, we seemed to have a happy extended family in Anathoth and I was welcome in it. Times are different now: no happy family, all are dead except me – the one they all hated.

It is hard not to feel nostalgic about those times, times of innocence and ignorance. I guess that is the trigger for writing this diary. It is intensely private, not even to be shared with Baruch who has written all the messages God has given to the people through me. It may never be finished, but I had to start it because of what happened today. Again, it was my birthday, and again, God spoke to me. Funnily enough, even after all these years of hearing his voice, it still startles me and thrills me – I could never fake it or imagine it. The burning shock of the voice of God within me; scorching but uplifting, frightening but joyous. A feeling that brings me to instant wakefulness or stops me in my tracks as I walk. And when the voice fades, the effects remain – God's demand for action continues to burn within me.[8] Yet today, once again, I was told "The Lord did not send you". It was Johanan the son of Kareah this time,[9] along with the other leaders of the pathetic remnants of the once great army of Judah. If only they could experience the voice of God! Then they would know I could never make it up. But they don't believe me. No-one ever has....

If only things could have turned out differently. King Josiah was the great comfort and hope of those of us who loved the Lord, Yahweh our God. Josiah, the Boy King, was probably the reason I was willing to agree when God told me his plans for my life, plans that had started before I was born.[10] But Josiah died, and with him died all hope that Judah might turn back to God. Memories are all I have left now, memories of a city once full of people, now sitting lonely and forlorn; memories of a family of priests who served at a temple now ground into the dust.

☙

March, 626BC – the 13th year of King Josiah

In Judah, we never made much of birthdays. If a young man ever suggested a celebration, the older priests would always remind him sternly of the only birthday feast mentioned in our Scriptures, where Pharaoh hanged his chief baker![11] Nevertheless, as Levites, our birthdays *were* important to us, and particularly to those of us who were destined to be priests. God had given rules about when we could start our life's work, so the date was important, even if having a party was not. My birthday was a little more special than most, because I shared a birthday with the king.[12] Was that another part of the pre-planning of God in my life? It certainly made the king very important to me, particularly his well-known search for godliness.

---

[8] Jeremiah 20:9

[9] Jeremiah 43:2

[10] Jeremiah 1:5

[11] Genesis 40:20-22

[12] This helps the story, but there is no evidence for it in the Bible.

My Birthday

Every year, my father would tell me, "Jeremiah, you are still only a young lad; too young for the work of God." But I knew how old the king was, and would sometimes ask cheekily "Does not King Josiah do the work of God?" Josiah was just four years older than I: he had become king when he was only eight, yet no-one doubted that he was doing the work of God. "Ah, yes," my father would reply in his rich, deep voice, "but he is only a king, while you will be a priest, appointed to work even between the king and our omnipotent God!"

My father's voice was just right for a priest. When he spoke, it made you feel as if he had all the wisdom of the ages at his disposal, and you were enveloped in the warm certainty of an endlessly glorious kingdom of Judah, with the temple in Jerusalem at its centre, and the priesthood of Aaron as Judah's guiding light.

Everyone loved my father, and they loved to listen to that delightful, caressing voice. But even before I turned seventeen, I was beginning to wonder about some of the murkier depths behind it.

On my seventeenth birthday, during our evening meal, he had reminded me as usual that I was still too young. Then, as I lay on my bed that night thinking and praying, my life's work was shown to me. If God ever speaks to you, it may be different, but for me, the word of God came like the slow start of a fire; with light and heat, and the knowledge that this was something very special. I don't think there was a light in the room, it was more as if the light was inside me and I could feel it. After a few seconds of this growing feeling of a presence within me, the voice came. Expansive, vast, uncontained, it seemed to fill my being, threatening to burst me open. Yet it was also calm, tranquil almost, as my God revealed his long-held plans for me:

> "Before I formed you in the womb I knew you,
> and before you were born I consecrated you;
> I appointed you a prophet to the nations."[13]

---

[13] Jeremiah 1:5

I'm not really sure whether I responded out loud or just spoke in my mind. How do you speak to a presence that fills you with sound, yet doesn't seem to make a sound? I had no doubt whose the voice was: "Ah, Lord God! I do not know how to speak, for I am only a youth." My father's words came very easily to me despite my feeling of irritation earlier in the day when he had used them. Again, the voice of God:

> "Do not say, 'I am only a youth';
> for to all to whom I send you, you shall go,
> and whatever I command you, you shall speak.
> Do not be afraid of them,
> for I am with you to deliver you,
> declares the Lord."[14]

It didn't seem strange to have God announcing who he was at the end of this speech. Rather, it was comforting, despite the surge of light within me, the surge of a white-hot flame filled with power and infinite purity. It was an experience I was to become very familiar with. Whenever God announced his name – Yahweh – the light inside me burned hotter and brighter, and the power in the voice seemed to swell. This was the great creator, the living God, speaking to me – within me – how could it be possible? These things didn't happen in modern times, yet here I was experiencing the voice of God; hearing a challenging command that came with a reassurance of the presence of God in my life!

Then suddenly everything changed. Instead of a voice inside me, there was now a vision clear as crystal before my eyes, as a hand which I somehow knew to be the hand of God, came shining from the darkness of the night and touched my mouth. Instantly I thought of Isaiah, the great prophet who, more than a century ago, had volunteered to be God's messenger.[15] His complaint of unclean lips had been swept away when they were touched by a burning coal taken from the very altar of God; even his sins had been taken away in that searing second.

---

[14] Jeremiah 1:7-8
[15] Isaiah 6

I had complained about being too young. Could the hand of God fix this also? But no, he declared that instead his words had been put within my mouth. The words of God – in *my* mouth? This was what I had often longed for – words of wisdom and certainty from God. It is strange to think back on this now, now that the certainty of God's message has brought me such trouble and suffering over the years, but if I had to choose again, I would still want his words within me, leading me as he wills it.

The voice had not finished; the sting in the tail was yet to come. At the tender age of seventeen, I was told:

> "See, I have set you this day
> over nations and over kingdoms,
> to pluck up and to break down,
> to destroy and to overthrow,
> to build and to plant."[16]

Humility was never my strong point, but even so, this left me utterly bewildered: how could *I* possibly be set over nations and kingdoms? How could I pluck up and break down? Even the great king Josiah was only set over one nation, one kingdom. I was a priest – or I would be once I grew up – not a prophet or a king. How could this ever be? And did I want it anyway? I remember clearly the jumble of my thoughts as the vision faded and the voice left me.

The darkness closed around me again and there was nothing left to show that God had ever been there in the room with me, touching me, changing me. Except, that is, for the burning urge that remained, the urge to do something, to read, to study, to talk, to pray. But how could I pray when God had been there inside? My prayers were always made to a God who was outside, a God who never replied to the jumbled thoughts I often chose to call 'prayer'. Would I ever be able to pray in an ordinary way again when I had actually talked with God?

But I must do something, and sleep was impossible. Maybe it would be best to think and try to remember all that God had said, or even write it all down.

---

[16] Jeremiah 1:10

In the end, that was what I did, and so started my habit of writing down the words God spoke to me. It was a good habit and most of the time I followed it. Only in my most stubborn times did I avoid the writing, and even those messages God ultimately forced me to write. Fighting with God never works – he always wins in the end. I suppose I am glad about that too – now.

Ten minutes of writing completed the job. I had no difficulty remembering exactly what God had said, and no difficulty understanding that this was a message no-one would ever believe. Apocalyptic for me, but apocryphal to everyone else. How could I ever convince my father? It wasn't hard to imagine his words, and the deep, somewhat mocking tone of voice as well – "My son, you are too young for God to use you in that way. Think of Moses – 80 years old before God could use him. And Elisha – bald as an egg before he could become God's prophet. I had to wait for God's time, and you must too." My father always had examples at his fingertips – but he always chose the ones he wanted and ignored the others. What about David, or Joash, or even King Josiah himself? Why ignore the young boy Samuel when God hadn't? But all the logic in the world wasn't going to help, and I knew it.

So what should I do? I spent the rest of the night wrestling with that problem. Sleep was still impossible; my feeling of a need to do something still overwhelmed me. But what? This had been the word of God. I couldn't ignore it just because no-one would believe me. Yet what to do anyway? The word of the Lord to me had only been information; a sort of job description and notice of appointment, but without a starting date or anything specific to work on. However, if God's spirit was urging me to do something… all I could think of was to do some research. I knew that once upon a time there had been scrolls of the books of Moses, but generations of evil kings had seen these destroyed or lost. What could I research? The night was long and filled with troubled thoughts before I slipped out of the house a little before dawn; eager to watch the sun rising in hope that a light would shine in my heart too, showing me which way to turn.

If only God would set up a test as he had with Aaron – selecting his priest by causing a dead stick to sprout and grow almonds so that everyone would recognise God's selection. If only… but everyone knows that God simply doesn't do things like that in modern times.

⳩

It was a beautiful sunrise, complete with a wonderful dance of shimmering clouds in ever-changing shapes and hues. A long thin cloud with strange protrusions had caught my attention, since it almost seemed to look like Aaron's almond rod, having grown leaves and fruit – and then the voice came:

"Jeremiah, what do you see?"[17]

I answered, "I see an almond branch", and God told me that I had seen well for he was watching over his word to make sure it happened. If you know Hebrew, you will know that our words for 'almond' and 'watching' are very similar. It was a play on words. I was learning unexpected things about the God I worshipped. But what did it mean? God watching words? Which words?

My confusion was pretty much complete as I dazedly watched the almond branch cloud slowly lose its shape as it moved across the sky to the north. I remembered the prophet Amos had been asked about what he saw when God showed him a plumb line.[18] Amos had been given many messages of judgement on Israel's neighbours – if I were to be a prophet to the nations, maybe these were the words God would be watching over to fulfil. I must go to Jerusalem and read the words of Amos again. One of the advantages of being from a priestly family is that it was easy to get access to the scrolls of the prophets, even the prophets from Israel like Amos. From memory, there were messages against Damascus, the Philistines,

---

[17] Jeremiah 1:11

[18] Amos 7:8 – A plumb line is a string with a weight on the end (called a plumb). When the string is held up it will form a vertical line and can be used to check that walls or posts are truly vertical.

Tyre and Edom, the Ammonites and... and maybe some others. The consistent theme of threes and fours made them much easier to remember, but had those prophecies been fulfilled or not? Did God still need to watch over those words or had the work already been done?

To me, there was a beauty in the thought of God speaking against nations and carefully watching his words as they flew like a burning arrow to the target – punishing the enemies of Israel. It was a simple mistake to make. Being appointed a prophet to the nations made me think that I would not be a prophet to my own people. Little did I know that it was my own people who would make my life a misery for so many years; my own people who would, just like the other nations, be the unresponsive target of God's fiery arrows of prophecy.

As the 'almond branch' cloud diffused to the north a sudden change came over the sky. Instead of clouds, all I could see to the north was what had the appearance of the lip of a giant cauldron superimposed on the clouds, filling the whole horizon, its seething and boiling contents tipping terrifyingly toward me. Again, the voice:

"What do you see?"[19]

Fear made my voice crack a little as I replied, "I see a boiling pot, facing away from the north." Then, as I struggled to fully absorb the words of the burning voice, God explained to me what this vision meant. A disaster was approaching from the north, an unspeakable catastrophe; all the nations of the north attacking God's holy city. The Lord would declare his judgements against Judah and Jerusalem because they had worshipped other gods.

And I was the one who had to tell my people.

My blood ran cold at the thought; I cringed inwardly at the idea of being the young upstart who told an entire city – an entire nation – that their worship was false! My father.... But... surely not even my father was as important as my

---

[19] Jeremiah 1:13

maker? And all the ungodly people in Jerusalem certainly needed this message; there was no question about that!

Still the voice of the Lord continued, insistently telling me that I must get ready for this work and promising to give me the mental strength I needed to keep going whatever the difficulties. He spoke with unforgettable word pictures:

> "I make you today a fortified city,
> an iron pillar, and bronze walls, against the whole land,
> against the kings of Judah, its officials, its priests,
> and the people of the land. They will fight against you,
> but they shall not prevail against you,
> for I am with you, declares the Lord, to deliver you."[20]

Now, there is another repeated feature of the words of God which was shown plainly here, but I was too overcome and too naive to notice it at the time: his simplest messages often include the most shocking, dangerous, complex or utterly overwhelming ideas. "Against...the priests". I was to be a priest; my father was a priest; my uncles were priests; some of my cousins were priests; my whole family were priests. Yet God's word was going to make me fight against them.

Had I been armed with the experience I now have of the words of Yahweh, this would have rung alarm bells immediately, but in those days I was ignorant of his ways – too ignorant, really.

---

[20] Jeremiah 1:18-19

Chapter 2

A Beginning

Had anyone else seen the bubbling pot? This was the question that filled my mind as I returned to my family home in the cool after dawn. The sight had been overwhelming, gigantic, filling half of the sky; completely obscuring the clouds shot through with the colours of sunrise. Surely shepherds in the fields and travellers abroad on the roads would have noticed? Or had this all been a vision, presented personally to me; visible only to me? But why? Why would God ever give a special vision to an unimportant seventeen-year-old lad? God was Master of the Universe, busy with the Control of the Nations, occupied with Kings and Leaders, far too busy to talk to me! It didn't make much sense to me then, and it honestly still doesn't − except that it shows how close God can be to each one of us, how involved in the lives of individuals, how incomprehensibly powerful and kind, that he will take the time to draw near to anyone who wants to draw near to him.

This was an indescribably important landmark in my life. God had *spoken* to me, and this was amazing enough in itself; but now God had given me *visions* as well. I knew that God had spoken to many important prophets in the past, men who were giants of faith and righteousness, men I had eagerly devoured stories about as a child, men I admired and wished I could know. But *me?* I wasn't in their class and I knew it; I couldn't be a great prophet like Samuel, a leader like Moses, a great father like Abraham. It just wasn't possible. And yet… somehow all this was happening. I stumbled blindly along the familiar path to our house as I mused over what was happening to me; wondering what God would do next, or what I should do next. I still had nothing to go on. "A prophet to the nations" was all very well, but a prophet needs something to say, and for me, that meant being told what to say. I guessed (or hoped!) that I would have to wait for God to spell out my task in detail. This was a most comfortable conclusion for me, since it put off the day when I would start the work God had described.

"Where have you been?" asked Azariah,[21] my oldest brother, as I tried to slip into the house unnoticed, still feeling unsure about what was really going on. Opportunity Number 1 – but there was never a chance I was going to take it. Just imagine: "Ah, yes, Azariah. I have just been given a vision from Yahweh warning that Judah will be destroyed by a nation from the north because we have been worshipping other gods." No. It couldn't possibly be done. Maybe later, once God had given more detail…. So instead I responded with what I hoped was a casual, "Out to see the sunrise".

But then, suddenly, it started; the slow kindling of the flame inside me, and I knew I had to get away from the rest of the family before God spoke. "Excuse me, I must go…" was all I had time for.

---

[21] Assuming that Jeremiah's father was the High Priest Hilkiah, Azariah would have been his older brother (1 Chronicles 6:13).

Dodging out of the door, I ran up the steps to the roof which was normally empty at that time of morning. By the time I reached the top step, I was being engulfed from within by a white-hot brightness which carried with it an indefinable feeling that God was displeased with what I had just done. Gladly, I saw that there was no-one else on the roof, and I hurried across to the opposite parapet, the side of our house which faced towards Jerusalem, obscured though it was by hills. I rested my hands on the rough stones as the words of God rushed over me like a wave of fire:

> "Go and proclaim in the hearing of Jerusalem,
> Thus says the Lord,
> 'I remember the devotion of your youth,
> your love as a bride,
> how you followed me in the wilderness,
> in a land not sown.
> Israel was holy to the Lord,
> the firstfruits of his harvest.'[22] "

Each word was a firebrand inside me, glowing and burning hot. As a child, I had wondered how prophets remembered what God had said to them so that they could write it down exactly, word for word; but now, I suddenly understood. Each word struck like a glowing nail, placed immovably in the wall of my mind. I could scan the wall in my mind's eye and read each word, words that never cooled or lost their brightness. This was God's answer to my comfortable feeling that I could put off the work he was giving me. As I looked, unseeing, towards Jerusalem, hidden as it was behind the higher ground of the Mount of the Watchmen[23] in the middle distance, God told me what I was to say there. There was no time to think about what I was being told: no time to understand. God was talking: I could but listen. Later would come the feeling of doom as I recognised the collision course on which God had placed me.

---

[22] Jeremiah 2:2-3

[23] Har Hatsophim (הַר הַצּוֹפִים), also called Mount Scopus, is to the north of, and slightly taller than the Mount of Olives.

A Beginning

> "Thus says the Lord:
> 'What wrong did your fathers find in me
> that they went far from me,
> and went after worthlessness, and became worthless?'[24] "

Everybody in Israel knows that we as a people have gone astray and worshipped other gods, so this was no surprise. But then…

> "And I brought you into a plentiful land
> to enjoy its fruits and its good things.
> But when you came in, you defiled my land
> and made my heritage an abomination.
> The priests did not say, 'Where is the Lord?'
> Those who handle the law did not know me;
> the shepherds transgressed against me;
> the prophets prophesied by Baal
> and went after things that do not profit.
> Therefore I still contend with you,
> declares the Lord,
> and with your children's children I will contend."[25]

It was getting alarmingly close to home. As I "read" these words in my mind later, I saw clearly the danger I was in. "Shepherds" must refer to leaders and kings and it was simply not safe to say anything against them. Times had changed from the dark days of King Manasseh,[26] but it was still not wise to say things against a king – even one as benevolent as Josiah. As for his nobles, they were much less benevolent. Moreover, a man may do dangerous things against leaders and still be protected by his family; but I would be attacking my family as well. How could I condemn the priests in this way? I had learned of God from my family, yet God was telling me that the priests did not know him. Had I learned wrongly myself? I resolved to re-read what scrolls I could find of the law, the prophets and the chronicles – if the priests did not know God, the only way I could get to know him better was to read his words.

---

24 Jeremiah 2:5

25 Jeremiah 2:7-9

26 2 Kings 21:16

But the real issue was: how could I deliver this message from God? Did God really mean what he was telling me to say, or was he using extreme language to get his people's attention? – maybe a bit like the prophet Jonah with his message that Nineveh would be destroyed in 40 days, a threat which God knew would never be fulfilled because of their subsequent repentance.[27] Maybe.

Overall, the message was just so damning, so horrible, so downright disgusting. I cringed as God likened my nation to eager prostitutes lusting after other men; like restless young camels in heat.[28] I didn't *think* it applied to me, but could I be sure? If my teachers did not know God, how could I know him as I ought? Maybe God found my worship offensive! How could I know? In the later musing of quiet hours, I thought I found my answer in the wise words of Manoah's very practical wife, when speaking with her frightened husband after an angel had told them about the coming birth of Samson.[29] She assured her husband that God would not kill them when he had just given them a message of immediate future events. God had told me that he would be with me to deliver me from those I would be speaking to. Surely he would not do this if I were worshipping him just as wrongly as those whom he was condemning? But I must get on with reading those scrolls again.

God's message went on and on, and none of it was reassuring or pleasant.

God's message; my message.

With absolute clarity I remember the struggle in my mind. There was no doubt that this message was from God. The fire inside me brooked no other explanation; but could I, Jeremiah, son of Hilkiah the High Priest of Israel,[30] deliver this message?

---

[27] Jonah 3 and 4

[28] Jeremiah 2:23-24

[29] Judges 13

[30] Jeremiah 1:1 tells us that Jeremiah was the son of Hilkiah, one of the priests in Anathoth. 2 Chronicles 34:9 tells us of Hilkiah the High Priest in the eighteenth year of the reign of Josiah, just 5 years after the start of Jeremiah's ministry. In neither case are we told who Hilkiah

I was terrified at the thought, and the more I thought of it, the more terrified I became. No one would listen; they would argue and ask for proof. I could imagine my father's imperious voice: "Jeremiah, you are still only a young lad, too young for the work of God; go back home and leave God's work to men." But I had heard the voice of God! How could I resist? There was no way out, no way to avoid the terror that would surround me. Yahweh, God of the universe, was leading me headlong to disaster, a disaster that had come on many of his servants the prophets. A half-forgotten story from the time of King Joash, almost 200 years before, was tugging at the corners of my memory; the story of how King Joash – mostly righteous until that time – had killed Zechariah the son of Jehoiada the High Priest because he did not like the message of God in Zechariah's mouth.[31] Would history repeat itself with me?

There seemed no point in dwelling any more on the sheer impossibility of the job, since I was going to do it anyway. Any other option was unthinkable: God had spoken; I was his servant; I must obey, and I did not want it any other way.

So when should I start? I knew intuitively that it wasn't going to get any easier if I waited, so I supposed that meant starting straight away. Today. After all, Jerusalem was only an hour's walk away. But what about my family? It didn't seem fair to let them find out about my work from others, or by suddenly hearing me speaking in the gates of Jerusalem. So I must tell them: right now. I took one last look toward Jerusalem, seeing in my mind's eye its streets and lanes, so full of people – people I must speak to – and breathed one last prayer, desperately asking my God for help in finding the best words to use. Then I retraced my steps down into the house, to find that almost nothing had changed.

---

was the son of. The "son of" formula was a common way of differentiating between people who shared the same names and is used often in Jeremiah. Since it is not used here, it may suggest that there was only one person of that name.

[31] 2 Chronicles 24:20-21

Azariah was still standing near the door as he had been when I had fled to the roof as I felt the power of Yahweh overshadowing me.

It was not really the time for musing on the working of time, but I remember the question rising in my mind, "Does the work of God always take as long as it seems to?" The message from God and my resulting thoughts must have filled at least fifteen minutes – yet here was Azariah still standing in the same place as he had been, and the subject under discussion didn't seem to have progressed much either. It was a common subject in our house – who would be going where today. This, of course, was just the perfect opportunity for me to tell my new plans for the day – God's plans.

Of course, God knew this very well, and I suppose that this was the reason for what appeared to be the delaying of the smooth flow of time. Another of the characteristics of God which I have learned over the years, is that things always work out more easily when I try to do his work immediately, rather than delaying or procrastinating. How I wish that I could have known some of God's earlier prophets, to see whether this is just the way God deals with me, or if it is more a principle of his operations with mankind. I suspect it is the latter. When God told Abraham to sacrifice his only son Isaac, Moses tells us that he made an early morning start to his journey,[32] heading for the same place that I was to go on this sunny morning. Had Abraham waited until later, would that sacrificial journey ever have begun? Starting would never have got any easier for him – or for Sarah.

I took a deep breath. "I am going to Jerusalem today", I said slowly. "Yahweh our God has spoken to me and given me a message for the people." God had made my job much easier; my father and mother were both in the room listening, and Azariah and Gemariah[33] my older brothers were there as well.

---

[32] Genesis 22:3

[33] Jeremiah 29:3 mentions Gemariah as the son of Hilkiah. Since it does not specify which Hilkiah, it seems most likely that there was only one Hilkiah – Jeremiah's father (Jeremiah 1:1).

The whole family could be told at one time, and how they responded was up to them.

Now this was most definitely not the common way in which I started a new day, so it was no surprise when my family looked at me for several seconds, open-mouthed and speechless. Azariah and Gemariah looked at each other and then at my father. My mother looked at me wide-eyed, but seemed to have an excited, pleased look. She was a godly woman, and any hint of God working in Israel filled her with happiness.[34] But in the end it would all come down to what my father said. He would carry the family with him, and most of the people as well. He looked thoughtful and took a few seconds to respond, while for me the world stood still. The fading warmth of the voice of God was still urging me to action, but I was used to the voice of my father as the ultimate authority. Even if God were to continue to take command of my life, clearly it would take a while to overcome this habit.

When my father spoke, his words were still thoughtful: "The voice of God, my son? You heard the voice of Yahweh? Is it possible? Is there really a God in Israel?" Reflective, but doubtful.

"Yes, father," I urged him. "There *is* a God in Israel and he has told me to speak to our people. I've got to remind them of our nation's joy in God's salvation when he first led us out of Egypt, but that since then we have gone after *worthless* gods and become worthless."[35]

"When did he speak to you – and how?" Still the doubt.

"Last night and this morning. His voice spoke inside me, burning like a fire, speaking with a certainty that was somehow terrifying, yet irresistibly attractive – it was like nothing I could ever have imagined."

"Were you awake, or was it just a dream?" Azariah took up the questioning, and his tone showed that he felt he already knew the answer.

---

[34] There is no evidence for this except Jeremiah's godly character.
[35] Jeremiah 2:1-5

"I was awake, Azariah – it was in the middle of my prayers last night that it started. But even if I hadn't been, I could never have slept through that! It made me feel more awake than I have ever done in my whole life. Hearing his voice was like being burned up inside, but enjoying it somehow. I can't explain it any more than that."

Gemariah seemed to be the only one who had actually listened to God's message, "'Become worthless'? But what about King Josiah's reforms and our national revival? Do they mean nothing?" he asked. "Are you sure this was from God? It doesn't sound right."

If I had known then what I know now, my answer would have been different, but at that time I believed the revival was genuine amongst the priests, the temple workers and even many of the people. So I answered, "I'm sure we are much better than we were in Manasseh's time, but just look at the high places, the Asherah[36] and the altars to Baal[37] that are still around. Why, just last week, King Josiah had to be present when they chopped down that altar to Baal in Jerusalem.[38] He had to be there, because otherwise nobody was willing to do it. That altar was being used, Gemariah, it wasn't just there for decoration."

In reality, the situation was much worse than I knew. Most of the people hated Josiah's reforms and the priests and princes were no better. Josiah was almost completely alone in his love of God, but he was also a determined young man – a leader who was to single-handedly delay the promised destruction of the nation by many years, solely as a result of his own humble righteousness.

---

[36] Asherah (also called Ashtoreth) was a goddess worshipped by the Canaanites, Syrians and Phoenicians as the consort of the god Baal.

[37] Meaning "Lord", Baal was the name given to the chief god worshipped in Canaan, Syria and Phoenicia.

[38] This work of purifying Judah and Israel started in Josiah's twelfth year and seems to have continued until the eighteenth year (2 Chronicles 34:3-8), while Jeremiah's prophesying began in Josiah's thirteenth year (Jeremiah 1:2).

A Beginning

Oh, to have once more the blissful ignorance of my youth, when I did not know the melancholy truth about the priesthood of Israel – of my own family.

"Gemariah, you are right," my father rejoined, "Jeremiah, this message you have must be reviewed by the elders of the people, and the elders of the priests, before you can even think about delivering it."

Harping on my youth again. It was to be expected… and it might have been reasonable if the message had come from anywhere other than from God. He continued: "You write down every word of the message and give it to me. I will take it to Jerusalem and arrange to have it reviewed. If it is acceptable, we can select a quiet place for you to read it to a small group of people to gauge the response. It wouldn't do to be hasty with a serious matter like this – especially with you being so young."

I had known this job would not be easy. But where should I go from here? God had not said I must go to Jerusalem *today*. Maybe having the message reviewed could be the best step to take. But God's words were still burning in me.

"Go and proclaim in the hearing of Jerusalem…"[39]

No option for review there; no delay suggested while a committee approved or rejected the word of God. The answer was clear to me, but with this clarity of understanding came the horrifying knowledge that God's word would become a sword between me and my family. A sword I could not control, causing pain and injury I could not wish for. My mother's pain-filled eyes told me that she knew what my answer would be even before I did. Mothers can be very wise.

"Father," I started, speaking slowly, "Father, I can't do what you ask. God has told me to go and proclaim his word to Jerusalem and I must obey. Surely you can see that?" I was looking at him pleadingly, praying silently that God would give him understanding of my dilemma and a willingness to back down in the face of God's expressed will.

---

[39] Jeremiah 2:2

My father's determination was untouched. "I cannot see why you will not write down the words you say you have received from God and let the elders review them. The elders will not take away the word of God; all they will do is stop you from making a fool of yourself by acting without sufficient thought."

There is no point in giving more detail of the discussion. It was long and painful for me, caught as I was between a rock and a hard place. No-one shouted, but no-one changed their mind either. If I was to go to Jerusalem today, it was to be in direct opposition to my father and my family. If I was to stay home, it must be in direct opposition to the command of God – unless I could find some other way to understand his words.

I couldn't – so I went to Jerusalem.

Chapter 3

Destination: Jerusalem

An easy walk in the warm sunshine of a spring morning is not always easy. Anticipation of trouble can dampen enjoyment, and I certainly anticipated trouble that day. My father had tried one last time to convince me not to go to Jerusalem, suggesting again that the elders review the words I was to speak. He was sure that "some of them" would be able to be delivered to an "appropriate audience". His words had the opposite effect from the one he hoped for: they gave me the answer I needed. God had told me that the "appropriate audience" was Jerusalem. No more. No less. He had also told me what to say – a mere "some" of his words would not do.

As I walked the winding path which followed the contours of the hills, I had to thrash out the first conflict of my work – children were to respect and obey their parents, weren't they? Yet God had commanded me to do something that my father did not want me to do, and I was now committed to doing it. Was this right? Would God work in this way – requiring disobedience to parents? How could I decide what was really

God's way? Did I know of any patriarchs, kings or prophets who had disobeyed their parents to obey God's commands?

I thought, but drew a blank. Maybe Noah had to resist his parents, but I was fairly sure the scripture didn't tell us either way. The closest example I could think of was Gideon, when God told him to break down his father's altar to Baal, build an altar to God and offer his father's bull on it.[40] After this escapade – undertaken at night because of his fear of the townsfolk's response, Gideon's father supported him when the people of the town wanted to kill him. As I climbed to the pass between the Mount of Olives and Har Hatsophim, I remember asking myself the question: Would my father support me? After some to-ing and fro-ing in my thoughts, I decided he would. Ah, the optimism of youth: I was wrong.

The other pressing problem was *where* to deliver God's message. How could I announce God's message to the people so that all Jerusalem would hear it? Alive with the bustle and gossip of travellers, and backing on to the busy markets, the city gates would have plenty of ears to hear – as long as my voice could be heard over the uproar. And that was when I started to have some small doubts. God's words were still with me, glowing brightly in my mind's eye as I thought of them. But what if the glow faded when I was surrounded by the throng, or when people started to sneer, laugh or jeer? The doubts grew. Would I be able to remember what God wanted me to say? Cresting the highest point of the saddle to the north of the Mount of Olives, I saw Jerusalem spread out below me – and that was the final straw.

„

I stopped, took out my writing equipment and sat down to write. Now it may seem strange to you that I would have carried a papyrus scroll with me, let alone a pen and ink, but I had already wanted to write down God's message before this attack of cold feet. Sometimes being prepared can make it much easier to lose faith. Other times, it is a lack of

---

[40] Judges 6:25-32

preparation that is the biggest threat to faith. Faith is so fragile. Ways of escape that don't require faith are so tempting.

The scroll I had brought was the scroll on which I had written God's first messages – could it really have been just last night? Looking down on the temple of God, I wrote out the words of God that I must deliver to the people of Jerusalem. A sudden lack of faith was not the best trigger for writing these words, but it was good to get them written down, and it gave me more time to think about God.

God had chosen Jerusalem in the time of King David, a little more than 350 years ago, and his beautiful house had been built by the great King Solomon. I could see the temple with its two massive bronze columns at the entrance and the giant flower-shaped bowls on top. A few people were passing in and out of the gates of the temple, but even from far away, the gates and buildings looked dilapidated and run-down. The columns showed a patina of age – where they weren't coated with decades of bird droppings; nothing in the temple reflected the sunshine since nothing was cleaned or polished.

Maybe God was giving me new eyes to see things from his point of view, for suddenly the contrast between the gleaming palace area and the squalid temple precinct stood out very clearly. Other areas of the city also gave the appearance of cleanliness and loving attention: these were areas where I knew there were pagan temples and where Josiah had recently begun his work of cleaning up the city – spiritually.

What a marvellous king was Josiah! Just eight years old when he started to reign, only sixteen when he started to impose his own will on his minders, overriding their desire to continue the status quo of worship. Josiah wanted to worship Yahweh, the God of our fathers, and he got his way while he was still considered a boy by many. He started to gather around him the few righteous men who had survived the murderous reigns of his father and grandfather. He listened to their advice and tried to learn the ways of God. Last year, at 20 years of age, his most determined steps had been taken, based on the knowledge of God growing in him. He began a purge. Altars and images to false gods were his targets, and he went to work with a vengeance. The most popular altars to Baal were cut down in his presence. High places to these abominable gods were destroyed and their so-called priests sent away in disgrace.

However, even a king needs to be a little cautious, as Rehoboam had found to his cost. Josiah was moving slowly, proclaiming his intentions and trying to carry the people with him. His plan would take several years to complete, but it had started well.

Unfortunately though, nothing had yet been done for God's house, which needed much work to restore it to the glory and purity of the past. Rather, the worship of God attracted few and God's house was left to the ravages of time, like a husband deserted by an unfaithful wife, left to fend for himself while she pursued a lover's more glamorous lifestyle. Israel was this unfaithful wife, not content with only one lover, but looking for an exciting life filled with the hedonistic worship of many gods.

These places of pagan worship were not safe harbours for widows; orphans found no safety within their walls, just exploitation and bestiality. This was the "freedom" Israel had sought: freedom from loving their neighbour, freedom from faithfulness and honesty, freedom from the protective guidance of God's love.

As I wrote out God's words and looked down on Jerusalem, the words made more sense to me, and I knew I would find it easier to deliver them with confidence. We *had* defiled God's land and made his heritage an abomination. The parts of the city used for evil were clearly cared for and popular. These were the places where money and effort were spent.

The temple area was still a haven for Baal worshippers, Asherah poles, pagan altars and the living quarters of vile perverts. All these were hidden in the temple area, busily used by those content to mix the worship of the one true God with the worship of meaningless idols. Although I did not know it at the time, even the good intentions of Josiah would not change this for another five years.

Now if Josiah, seemingly a good and righteous young king, was doing nothing about the temple, surely he must be ignorant of the secret things that happened there? If he was cutting down altars to Baal elsewhere in the city, yet leaving the same altars in the dark corners of the temple of God to continue their sordid operations, surely he must not know about them? So just who were the people in control, hiding these things from the King? Who didn't want these things to be known or changed – and why?

I would learn the answers to these questions all too soon.

Chapter 4

"Speak to Jerusalem"

The tawny walls of Jerusalem loomed above me as I walked toward the Benjamin Gate.[41] Market stalls had spilled out of the city and lined the road to the walls with drab tents, shouting hawkers and colourful merchandise, whilst the bleating of sheep and goats filled the air. Mingling with the mid-morning crowd, I passed through the gate under the watchful eye of the guards and into the sheep market within. Immediately a figure moved towards me – clearly he had been waiting for my arrival. It was Hanamel, my cousin.

"Jeremiah," he greeted me, "Shalom."

"Shalom, Hanamel. What brings you here? Sheep aren't normally your chosen companions!"

"No, nor yours," he replied, smiling a little awkwardly.

---

[41] The Benjamin Gate is referred to twice in Jeremiah (37:12-13 and 38:7). Jeremiah 20:2 also refers to the upper Benjamin Gate of the temple, which may be the gate of the temple right near the city gate of the same name. Some believe it is the Sheep Gate referred to in Nehemiah and in John's gospel.

"I suppose not, but it is a popular place, and that's what I need today."

"Ah, yes," he replied, constraint in his voice. "That's what I'm here to talk to you about. You have some so-called message from God, I hear."

"No, Hanamel, not 'so-called'. But yes, I do have a message from God which I must deliver to his people."

"Would you like to come and tell me the message?" He motioned encouragingly with his hands. "We could go to our uncle's[42] house and you could fill me in on the details."

"Who asked you to do this?"

"Well…your brother, Azariah." Hanamel spoke a little sheepishly.

That explained why Azariah had left in a hurry after the end of our family discussion this morning.

I tried to be gentle but definite: "Hanamel, if you had been told what to do by Yahweh our God, what would you do if someone tried to distract you and delay you?"

"What do you mean?"

"You were sent to stop me from delivering God's message to Jerusalem; to keep me occupied with talking to my family and friends instead of speaking to these people here." I motioned to the crowd around us. Busy as they were with their sheep and goats, they were unlikely to listen to any message from God, even if it were delivered by an angel. However, this was the work God had assigned me and I couldn't justify a delay.

"But, Jeremiah, is it really so urgent? Do you really need to do this today? What about tomorrow, after discussing it with others? The message won't change just because you wait until tomorrow. You don't want to upset too many people…" his voice trailed off as he looked around. And well he might, for within earshot were the guards in the gate, the watchmen on the walls, the bustling crowds buying sheep and goats, the

---

[42] There is no evidence for this shared paternal uncle.

nodding worshippers facing several small shrines to various gods nearby, and behind us, the temple gates with their guards.

"Of course I don't want to upset people, but which is worse: upsetting people or upsetting God?" I felt that I was on firm ground here, as I had dwelt on this question many times over the last few years. This had been a source of disagreement in our family – me against the rest, with my mother abstaining. I had never had any doubts, although following through in practice is never quite so easy.

"Surely the elders should be able to guide us in matters of worship?" Hanamel asked the question I had heard so often before from my family. Very logical it seemed, except that everyone seemed to forget that Judah had not worshipped God properly for at least 70 years. The elders did not know God: that was exactly what God had been telling me this morning.

"No, Hanamel," I replied. "The elders do not know God. How could they? We have all heard what King Manasseh did to anyone who promoted the worship of Yahweh. Anyone who tried to serve the God of our fathers was slaughtered mercilessly." The corollary to this was something I did not see clearly until later: the survivors of Manasseh's purges were those who worshipped other gods, or who were at least willing to quietly fit their worship of God around the worship of other gods.

"I suppose you might be right," he responded slowly, doubtfully. Respect for elders has always been very important in Judah, and this conclusion threatened it.

I felt a little sorry for Hanamel. He was the son of my father's brother Shallum[43], and just a couple of years younger than I. We had often spent time together, growing up in Anathoth. Clearly he had been sent by "them" to stop me; take me away from my work; delay me. But it was not my work, it

---

[43] Hanamel was the son of Shallum (Jeremiah 32:7). Since his land was in Anathoth, a town of the priests, it is assumed that he was a priest, and thus a paternal rather than a maternal uncle. This may be supported also by Jeremiah 35:4, which mentions Maaseiah the son of Shallum as the keeper of the threshold of the house of God.

was God's work. It seemed very likely that he would get into trouble if he failed; but I couldn't let the plan succeed.

"Sorry, Hanamel, I can't come with you now. I will have a busy day today. God has told me I must deliver a message from him to the people of Jerusalem. I'm starting here and then I will go to some of the other gates. You are welcome to stay and listen – the message is for you too."

Hanamel tried a little longer to convince me, but finally he gave up and stepped away to watch and listen. I couldn't help wishing I could do the same!

CR

So now here I was, in the market near the gate, just where I had planned, ready to do God's will. But – how to start? Where to stand exactly? Should I warn the nearby stall holders? The urge to act was still with me – the after-effect of the voice of God – and Hanamel's presence also meant that I felt under pressure to start without delay. While talking, Hanamel and I had moved to a quieter corner, to a stall that normally sold sheep skins, but was now empty: the owner must have left early this morning. One of the boxes on which he normally spread his wares was right next to me, and I climbed up onto it. I made sure my scroll was in easy reach, just in case I got lost in the middle of my message, and then I started to "read" the words of God from the wall of my mind. I could still see all that was happening around me, but somehow the words were visible too. It is very hard to describe, but the one who makes the eye can also make eyes see things differently when he wants to. I took a deep breath, asked God to make me strong and keep guiding me, and then spoke as loudly as I could:

"People of Jerusalem, hear the word of Yahweh your God.
'Thus says the Lord,
"I remember the devotion of your youth,
your love as a bride,

how you followed me in the wilderness,
in a land not sown." '44 "

As soon as I started to speak, the hagglers and vendors nearest to me suddenly began to turn around and look and listen. While my voice doesn't have the rich and comforting overtones that make my father's voice so beautiful, it has always been reasonably powerful – and maybe the sharp edges made it easier to hear in the Sheep Gate market that day. Or maybe it was God's work. Whatever the reason – and it can be very hard to tell when God works! – in a very short time, I had quite an audience crowding round. No hecklers yet, but then, I hadn't got to anything unpleasant yet.

" 'Israel was holy to the Lord,
the firstfruits of his harvest.
All who ate of it incurred guilt;
disaster came upon them,
declares the Lord.'45 "

An audience in Jerusalem was always going to like the message that Israel was special to Yahweh and under his protection. Even the scattered few from the northern kingdom – easy to identify due to the slightly foreign look of their clothing – would like to hear that message. God's next words included them too:

"Hear the word of the Lord, O house of Jacob,
and all the clans of the house of Israel.
Thus says the Lord:
'What wrong did your fathers find in me
that they went far from me,
and went after worthlessness, and became worthless?'46 "

"What do you mean by that, young man?" asked a man nearby, suspiciously. Should I answer him, or continue with my message? A quick thought showed that the next words might be taken as an answer, so I continued:

---

44 Jeremiah 2:2
45 Jeremiah 2:3
46 Jeremiah 2:4-5

"God answers your question, just listen:
'They did not say, "Where is the Lord
who brought us up from the land of Egypt,
who led us in the wilderness,
in a land of deserts and pits,
in a land of drought and deep darkness,
in a land that none passes through,
where no man dwells?"
And I brought you into a plentiful land
to enjoy its fruits and its good things.
But when you came in, you defiled my land
and made my heritage an abomination.'[47] "

Pausing, I saw growing disapproval, even hostility on the faces of many in the audience.

"An abomination? That's a very strong word, young 'un," said one dubiously. Others nodded.

Another was more antagonistic: "Defiled the land? Who do you think you are to abuse us like this?"

"You upstart, why should we listen to you?" yelled another.

Hanamel, who had been edging away as I spoke, now broke away from the gathering crowd and disappeared down the street. At that moment, things looked black, but I couldn't believe God would give me a job to do and allow me to be beaten up or killed before it was finished. I stood up straight, and tried to keep the fear out of my eyes as I returned their stares.

"We worship the gods as our priests and kings tell us, and all the prophets agree," shouted a man standing directly in front of my perch. "What do you say about that?"

"Yahweh says to you:

'The priests did not say, "Where is the Lord?"
Those who handle the law did not know me;
the shepherds transgressed against me;
the prophets prophesied by Baal
and went after things that do not profit.

---

[47] Jeremiah 2:6-7

> Therefore I still contend with you,
>> declares the Lord,
> and with your children's children I will contend.
>> For...'[48] "

A man, well-dressed in clothes of a faintly foreign cut – I guessed him to be from one of the cities of Israel – joined the crowd around me and interrupted me, calling out, "We've got to keep up with the times. In the nations around, and even in the towns of Israel where I come from, there are other gods being worshipped. We need to fit into our environment, mould our culture around the great cultures of the world. Learn their gods and make them our own so that we can gain strength from them. What good has Yahweh ever done us? Have you looked at the ruined cities in Israel?"

Once again, the next words God had given me were just right for this man:

> " '...cross to the coasts of Cyprus and see,
>> or send to Kedar and examine with care;
>>> see if there has been such a thing.
>>> Has a nation changed its gods,
>>> even though they are no gods?
>> But my people have changed their glory
>>> for that which does not profit.
>>> Be appalled, O heavens, at this;
>>> be shocked, be utterly desolate,
>>>> declares the Lord,
>> for my people have committed two evils:
>>> they have forsaken me,
>>> the fountain of living waters,
>>> and hewed out cisterns for themselves,
>> broken cisterns that can hold no water.'[49] "

I was amazed. The crowd had actually calmed down, despite the words of condemnation God was measuring out to them. Somehow, the interruption by the Jew from outside Judah had taken the angry feel from the air. My listeners all

---

[48] Jeremiah 2:8-9
[49] Jeremiah 2:10-13

had Judah's sense of holy superiority over the northern kingdom, which had completely abandoned the worship of Yahweh. I could see their indignation ease as they applied my words to these 'foreigners', rather than to themselves. Never mind: I was sure that it would return as they heard more of God's priceless, but oh, so painful, words....

I continued to deliver the priceless but painful message of Yahweh. Whenever I was interrupted, the interruption always seemed to fit the next words God had crafted for me to deliver. To say that I was awestruck would be no exaggeration. Yahweh had given me the words to speak and had made them fit perfectly the situation in which they would be delivered! I had always felt a deep respect for the power of God, but never had I felt so clearly that he was in total control of everything. If only I could make my audience feel the same awe and see how desperately they needed to worship God and him alone.

It took me about half an hour to deliver God's words near the Sheep Gate that spring morning.[50] No one stoned me. No one screamed abuse at me. No one compelled me to stop. Hardly anyone even walked away. But had anyone been affected enough by the words to see a need for immediate change? Even the parts I had found utterly repugnant, even these had passed seemingly unnoticed by my audience.

However, towards the end, some particularly well-dressed men had come to the edge of the crowd. The golden earrings and heavily embroidered borders of their garments showed wealth, while the neatly trimmed hair and beards suggested high positions. No-one had greeted them, but the people nearest to them had deferred to them and made sure they had a clear view through the crowd. I wondered who they were, wondered what they were there for. When I finished, they made no comments and asked no questions, they simply walked away with the crowd opening deferentially in front of them.

Business must always go on, and the stall-holders around me were eager to catch up with any business they might have missed out on in the previous half-hour. Within just a few

---

[50] The message referred to is taken from Jeremiah 2:2 – 3:5.

seconds, the crowd had dispersed, the voices extolling the virtues of sheep from Bethlehem or Bethel rose again, and God's message seemed to have sunk without trace in a pool of apathy. The message which had caused me so much soul-searching and worry, had garnered no response at all, and I was stunned. "You have polluted the land with your vile whoredom"; "you have done all the evil you could" – these were not words I could ever have shrugged off without response, yet here I was, alone, with no repentant throng, nor yet an angry, belligerent throng; just a busy, indifferent throng. It had all seemed to start so well, worryingly well in fact. People had been listening, responding, even fuming. But then the response had become lukewarm and unemotional. I supposed that I should really be glad, but I wasn't. I simply couldn't believe it.

"Excuse me, sir, could I please unpack my stall again?" The owner of the stall from which I had presented Yahweh's judgements had returned and wanted to get back to business.

It hardly seemed worthwhile after the first indifferent reception, but God's command had demanded more than just one announcement of his word, so I went to the other end of the city, finding my way to the Potsherd Gate, with its exit to the Valley of the Son of Hinnom.[51] There, amongst the many sellers of pots and pottery, I found another empty stall, with another wooden box normally used for displaying goods. Again I climbed onto the box so that God's words would not be missed by any who would be willing to hear. Again there was an immediate negative response. Again it seemed to fade away as God's word became more and more censorious. People interrupted in different places, but still the text God had given me to deliver seemed to fit exactly, the interruptions raising questions that were answered immediately by the very next stanza of God's music of reproach. It had amazed me the first time; it filled me with speechless awe the second. How could

---

[51] Jeremiah 19:2

God achieve this so perfectly? It was a small compensation for my overall disappointment with the response to Yahweh's message of condemnation and love. My nation did not care.

By this time, it was early afternoon, still only about six hours from the time when Yahweh had written these glowing, in-erasable words in my mind. The urge to act was wearing off, and visiting another three places was a difficult task, but I had to make sure that I spoke to as many of the people of Jerusalem as possible.

Each time I spoke in a new location, the well-dressed men appeared after a short while. Not once did they speak to me; not once did they speak to anyone in the crowd. Each time I counted them: six mysterious men. Each time I finished, they walked quietly away.

Who were they?

Chapter 5

Family Repercussions

That afternoon I felt rather mixed up as I left Jerusalem. The way home took me out through the Benjamin Gate, the site of my first attempt to warn the people of Jerusalem. As I walked through the market there, some of the men packing up stalls glanced at me with recognition, but no one accosted me or exchanged words. The guard had changed during the afternoon, so there was no recognition there, and I walked away from Jerusalem as if nothing special had happened at all.

Yet something very special had happened that day – for my nation, and for me. God had sent a prophet to his people, and his words showed that there was a monumental need for change. History could not be re-written, but the future was ours to shape, and God had shown us just how we needed to shape it. Idols must go and so must our ignorance of God's laws. So how could I get people to listen? During the day I had been heard by many of the people of Jerusalem, but none of the vital response had come. My words on this day had not seemed to strike the chord that must be struck. People must listen. How could I make them do so?

In some ways I was quite pleased with the way I had done my work. God's words had been repeated five times and I had not stopped, or run away, or backed down in any way from his message. This had been one of my chief fears, and it was a matter of great satisfaction that God had fulfilled his promise to me: "I make you today a fortified city, an iron pillar, and bronze walls[52]". He had also commanded me not to be afraid of them, and I had done this also.

Overall, though the message had not got the response I had hoped for, I felt that the day had gone well.

After crossing the Kidron Valley and taking the fork that led to Anathoth and beyond, I climbed the saddle and passed between Har Hatsophim and the Mount of Olives. Late afternoon had brought the quick cooling of early spring, and the sun slid smoothly down behind Har Hatsophim.

It appeared that the work of a prophet was not going to be too bad: God would protect me as he had said, and maybe my people would turn to God with such a revival as had never before been seen in Israel. Maybe the success of Jonah was possible! Niggling doubts were swept under the optimistic carpet of youth and I was looking forward to enjoying my mother's peerless cuisine.

Darkness was filling the valley below me as I climbed the hill to Anathoth. Our house was high on the hill and commanded a view towards the Jordan Valley and the mountains of Moab beyond – a stunningly beautiful view at times. Tonight, the sun had fallen behind the hills to the west, and traces of pink outlined the clouds. In the east, the mountains of Moab were sinking into night and the beauty of their faint grey ranks softly confirmed the feeling of contentment that filled me. God had called me, and God was in control.

How blind could I possibly be?

---

[52] Jeremiah 1:18

I had barely put my foot inside the door when it started.

"Here's the grand prophet, come to minister to his family!" said Azariah, sarcastically. Oldest brothers....

"Too grand to help with the housework"; Gemariah next.

"...and too grand to obey his parents!" My father. This was serious.

My mother made sure she was busy supervising the final preparation of the delightful meal I had been dreaming about, and would not look at me. The others made up for it by giving me all of their attention.

"Where did you get those words, Jeremiah, my son?" asked my father, " 'Those who handle the law did not know me.'[53] You were speaking of your relatives; your family; your friends: condemning us all. How could you do it?" He sounded hurt, but not angry.

"Father, I had to deliver the words of Yahweh, and those words are what he told me to say."

"How did he tell you?"

So I explained the events of the night, the fire of God's word within me and the signs of the early morning. I told of the job God had given me as a prophet to the nations. They tried to understand, but it was all too unreal to them. For them, God was really only a form of worship, not a living God who could fill you with his brightness or demand your instant attention and obedience. What proof could I give? As far as they were concerned, my messages from God were just vivid dreams and pictures imagined in fast-moving clouds. Neither my father nor my brothers could ever have changed the ordered direction of their lives on such a basis. For them a burning bush would have had a natural explanation and the call of mundane daily life would never have allowed God a real foothold in their plans.

It's funny, really: I was the one who could already believe in God as a living God without the proof he had shown me

---

[53] Jeremiah 2:8

today, while my family were the ones who seemed to need the proof – but couldn't see it. Only my mother, who had taught me to trust Yahweh from the beginning, seemed to have an inkling of how I felt.[54] My mother was the one who had told me all the old thrilling stories of Abraham, Isaac and Jacob as I curled up in her lap begging for more. In her mouth, Ruth became a shining example of faith in a God who lived and loved. From her stories, I knew King David as a friend who had gone for a while, but who would return to see his God in his flesh. Her stories, and the way she told them, had laid the foundation of the love of Yahweh indelibly within my heart. But then again, she had told the same stories to Azariah and Gemariah without having that effect on them....

So why was their assessment of God so different from mine? Why had God always been so real to me: utterly essential, sovereign and alive? Why could God only ever be a *part* of the fabric of their lives; to be adjusted, or trimmed to shape as required, to fit around the more important parts?

I still don't know why the difference was there, but it weighs heavily on me that, if only I could have convinced my family about what God is really like, maybe some of them would still be alive today. If only.

Mother supervised the serving of the evening meal as we argued. In those days, we always had plenty of servants around, and we tended to treat them more as furniture than as people. But on this one point our parents were insistent: we were not allowed to have loud arguments in front of the servants. But my actions that day broke through their caution, and frustration ran high. Azariah was scathingly contemptuous of my "so-called revelations", Gemariah was dubious, and Father was embarrassed, disappointed and angry. Mother – Mother was just confused. Her husband was her lord, but God was her true Lord, and she clearly believed me more than anyone else. It was three against one, yet with God's promise of strength holding true, I was able to quite calmly and

---

[54] Very little information is given about Jeremiah's mother and her name is unknown. Jeremiah 15:10 seems to suggest that Jeremiah cared about upsetting her by being the target of unrelenting criticism.

effectively refute their arguments. As for the servants – they would have plenty to tell their families when next they had the opportunity. Arguing, almost shouting and fighting – and in the High Priest's house at that! An upstart son, showing scant respect for his father, and criticising all of the priesthood. Unheard of! Unfortunately, they would soon hear much more than this.

I suppose we were very rich in those days[55], and all enjoyed the comforts that riches bring. How does a High Priest become rich? If you have lived in Israel, you will know how things are, and how money can stick to people's fingers. If you haven't, I won't answer that question now. The truth is that I didn't know the answer at that time either – being rich was completely natural for me, since we had been rich throughout my short life. Yet being rich had put a strait-jacket on every individual in our family when it came to talking about God.

The meal was deliciously tasty and piping hot; the company was bitter and cold. Silver plates held a variety of tempting foods, limited only by God's laws of cleanliness; stony hearts thought unattractive thoughts and made unpalatable plans, many of which were in no way limited by God's laws. Cups were filled with sweet wine which flowed freely; the conversation was tightly constrained and held nothing sweet. The smooth, deep, attractive voice of my father was only to keep up appearances for the listening servants.

The long and stressful evening ended with me going to my bed, exhausted. God's flame in me was flickering and fading, and the reaction was setting in. How much would be different because of this day? Would I ever go back to the life I led before? What would happen next?

---

[55] It is very likely that Hilkiah was rich based on the provision, by him and two other chief officers, of 2,600 Passover lambs and 300 bulls for the celebration of the Passover in 2 Chronicles 35:8.

Chapter 6

What Now?

There were no interruptions to my sleep that night, and a night's sleep can do much to ease the worries of a young man.

Early the next morning, I was huddled on the hillside revelling in another chilly sunrise. I was still excited by the idea that God had spoken to me but struggling to fathom his reasoning in making that choice. "Why me?" was the question that still filled my mind – whenever I wasn't dwelling on the mechanics of how I should respond to God's commands. Another sunrise gave me more time to think about this. The wonders of clouds tinged with pink and orange filled the sky again, with probing sunbeams edging the clouds with the gold of the presence of God: indescribable beauty given as a gift by God to all who chose to see. Sunrises and sunsets have always been a source of inspiration to me. In the majesty of the unveiling and re-veiling of the sun I can always find the loving presence of God, while also seeing the overarching primacy of Yahweh as creator: near, but ever so far above my human thoughts. When I feel lost, sunset and sunrise can always help me to find balance. When I have the choice, I will watch both each day – times of uplifting prayer for me.

Of course, in spring, the weather around Jerusalem is much less predictable than at other times of year, and many a spring morning is filled with the spring rain which we call the "latter rains" – often delivered with squally winds from God's storehouses.[56] Yet God had granted me two perfect sunrises in a row in which to marvel at his work in the world. And then suddenly it struck me: there had been none of the normal spring rain this year. Wasn't that just what I had been repeating to the people yesterday? God's voice had spoken about Israel's faithlessness and said:

> "Therefore the showers have been withheld,
>> and the spring rain has not come;
>> yet you have the forehead of a whore;
>> you refuse to be ashamed."[57]

Wrapping my cloak warmly around me, I lay on the hillside with the dawn of a new day unfolding around me, my mind free to contemplate my perverseness: I could confidently proclaim to everyone that God's words were completely reliable in every detail, while still feeling illogically surprised when I realised them to be true in one specific detail!

If I were to be a prophet to the nations, I would need to get used to this and be able to proclaim God's news of the future to my audience with a cohesive certainty. Elijah had showed no signs of surprise when fire fell from heaven and burned up the altar he had so newly repaired.[58] Even as the fire fell, his thoughts had already moved on to what he had to do next – killing the false prophets.[59] I must become like Elijah: God's announcements were certain and I must always present them as such. If my faith was weak and confused, how could I ever convince others to have an authentic faith? I suddenly understood that God's work depended as much on what I *was,*

---

[56] Jeremiah 10:13; 51:16
[57] Jeremiah 3:3
[58] 1 Kings 18:36-39
[59] 1 Kings 18:40

as on what I did. It felt like a massive extra weight of responsibility. There was no doubt that I was going to need all the help God had promised me (could it really have been just yesterday morning?):

> "...I make you this day a fortified city,
> an iron pillar, and bronze walls"[60]

Did I still want the job God had given me? At that time, the answer was a very definite "Yes". Although I did not feel myself qualified to do the work, I certainly wanted it done, if God said that it was needed. If his choice was that I should do it, then that was all there was to it. When I look back on the actions and decisions of that young man that was me, I see clearly the hand of God touching his heart, and his eagerness to have it so.

That morning the sun seemed to rise particularly slowly. The colours ebbed and flowed majestically across the sky, while the swallows darted and swooped around me. Families of rock badgers emerged from their homes as the sun's warming rays began to play over the rocks, and I was free to alternately revel in the beauty of creation and ponder my changed life.

Last night while communing with God on my bed before exhaustion and sleep had claimed me, I had developed a plan for this new day: Day Two of my work as a prophet. Jonah had prophesied for just one day, with astonishing success. I had preached for one day and had no obvious success at all, but maybe the message would spread and success would come through this. However, I had decided that even if there seemed to be no result, I would still continue speaking to the people of Jerusalem every day for one whole week. After seven days, I should have been able to deliver God's message directly to a significant percentage of the population of Jerusalem, and surely the rest would hear reports from others. Some quick calculations suggested that yesterday God's word would have been heard by about one to two thousand people – although most would not have listened to all of it. If I could continue to speak five times each day to an audience of about 200-400

---

[60] Jeremiah 1:18

people, then after seven days, about 7,000-14,000 people would have heard enough to be able to decide for themselves whether to believe it as God's warning word, or dismiss it as unimportant.

What I had not been able to decide was how I could be free to speak to the people at all! Until now, my days had been filled with studying the law and learning to be a priest. Yesterday, I had simply ignored this in the heat and enthusiasm of the word of God, but now the question needed to be answered, not just ignored. Did God mean this to be a full-time occupation for me? Was this just a week's work, or an ongoing responsibility? Must my schooling stop, and if so, what would my parents say?

My father had often said to us boys: "My sons, we are the teachers of Israel. We have the words of God to pass on to the people." In Judah, education has always had a high priority, and there were special expectations for the sons of priests and Levites. Over the course of my life, these expectations have fluctuated. The reformed king Manasseh wanted priests and Levites to lead the re-education of the nation, while Amon wanted none of that. Josiah actively encouraged religious education and based it directly on God's word. His sons and grandson left all training about God to an uncaring and ignorant priesthood. They had been so blessed with it themselves, but preferred to walk in other ways. Education leads and many will follow its leading, but it doesn't force. If it did, there could never be reformation. The ways of God would have died out from the earth long ago. After all, even some of the forefathers of Abraham were pagans.

Under God's laws, priests were important in the education of the nation. God said they must lead the Levites and the people, knowing the laws and how to apply them practically. Over the generations, large numbers of knotty problems have also been sorted out, and the High Priests and their sons were meant to know all of this case law very well. I knew much of it, but was still learning, and was not always very satisfied with the conclusions. However, would God want me to abandon this pursuit of studying the practical application of his laws in his nation? We Jews love to consider the minute details of real or imagined situations, and much of our training centred around studying the considered opinions and interpretations of various ancient experts, some of which were clearly nonsense. My brother Azariah revelled in the minutiae, while Gemariah was less enthusiastic but still willing to honour the words of those ancients. I felt that this "wisdom" often completely missed the point of God's laws. Would God prefer me to study his law directly and learn from him, instead of from opinionated but ignorant old men? Respect must be shown to the aged, but God is the oldest of all and the wisest of all – surely I must listen to him first?

All I was doing was wavering back and forward without progressing towards any solution to my conundrum: work as a prophet, or work as a priest? Which must come first? Anyone could be a prophet if God called him, but not all could be priests. Nobody was constrained from doing God's work as a prophet – or prophetess – but who could help to lead the priesthood to God better than a priest who was inspired by God to do so? Could I fill both roles at once? What would God want?

When God first appointed priests, he meant them to teach his law to the people. Unfortunately, the ancient original scrolls had all worn out or been destroyed. The copies we had now were of varying ages, but few were very old. God's words in the scrolls of Moses, David and other prophets had often fed Manasseh's bonfires, and we could no longer trace the history of God's words through each scroll ever copied. Don't get me wrong, we had many scrolls of portions of the law and many scrolls with instructions for its interpretation; but could we rely on them? My father and brothers thought me rebellious, and maybe they were right, but I wanted proof that these scrolls which claimed to be the word of God really were what they claimed. The High Priest was the final arbiter of what God's word said and what it meant, but I knew enough of the scrolls we had to see that they were very much a mixed bunch – some were authentic and accurate copies of older scrolls, while others were distorted copies, travesties of God's truth. Although I was no expert, it was obvious to me that we needed to do a lot of work to purge the rubbish from our libraries. For me, I still had much to learn, and my father wanted me to continue with my schooling.

According to tradition, the Levites were under the control of the sons of the High Priest, and my education was about to move in this direction, but God had said I was to be "a prophet to the nations".

How would I decide? Could anyone give me wise advice? It was a strange situation to be in: normally one would seek advice from a priest about such a matter, but I could not do so.

☙

In the end, after arguing around and around in circles without coming to any conclusions, I sat down and wrote the words God had said to me, and added some of my reactions:

- "A prophet to the nations" – supervising Levites did not seem a necessary skill if this was to be my job.

- "Do not say 'I am only a youth'" – if God had wanted me to finish my education first, all he had to do was wait longer before talking to me. Instead, he had said I must not worry about being young – and to me, that had to include not having finished my schooling.

- "To all to whom I send you, you shall go" – being prophet to the nations would mean travelling, and travel took time. Schooling could not fit in with this either.

- "Do not be afraid of them for I am with you..." – I had to fear God and go his way, rather than fearing my family and friends.

Having gone through this process, I had no doubts left. My classmates would have to go on learning without me. Jerusalem would hear God's word again today.

Chapter 7

King Manasseh

Every activity has a beginning;
Each tragedy, a time to strike;
Every kingdom, an ending.

A Jewish proverb[61]

For Judah, King Manasseh was the beginning of a tragedy that led inevitably to the horrifying death of a nation. In this world, evil is always there for people to choose, but some people take to it more naturally than others. Manasseh took to evil like a rat to food scraps from a very young age.

---

[61] Made up for the purpose.

Some work hard to achieve their goals in life, overcoming all obstacles along the way through sheer determination and relentless hard work. This is less common in an hereditary line of rulers, since the comfortable life of royalty often saps the drive to achieve, but Manasseh was not softened one whit by a life of ease. He was a driven man, from what I have heard; a man who pursued his goal tirelessly, rising early, staying up late, driving himself and those around him in a relentless struggle to overcome any resistance. And his target was evil. Nothing could satisfy his appetite for it.

King Manasseh's vision was a Judah famous for its idolatry, immorality and violence. Every day was an opportunity for progress.

Before he had reigned 20 years, King Manasseh had filled Jerusalem from one end to the other with idols, high places and shrines to the empty, useless gods of the surrounding nations.[62] He wooed the people away from God; he commanded the worship of Baal; he gave special tax reductions to those who helped with the construction of carved images and altars. He cajoled, he threatened, he led by example. Parties served him well, and many simple people took their first steps along the promiscuous path of Baal at street parties funded by the king. Drinking was encouraged. So were singing and dancing. Immorality flourished. Early opponents were lampooned; later opponents were exterminated.[63]

Every day, Manasseh would call his fortune tellers[64], who would use omens to decide his plans for the day. Honestly, who would let his life be controlled by the self-interested lies of sycophantic flunkies who cut up animals to "read the future"? Maybe Manasseh never noticed that his "experts" would always talk to him for some time before reading the omens for him. It is, after all, so much easier (and safer) to tell the king what he should do once you have found out what he wants to do! Of course, this too highlights the difference between Yahweh, the God of Israel and these superstitions: he

---

[62] 2 Kings 21:3
[63] 2 Kings 21:16
[64] 2 Kings 21:6

commands, and is never sycophantic. When people ask for an answer from Yahweh, they do not automatically get the answer they want to hear. That was what got me into trouble with Johanan and triggered my writing of this diary – he had already decided the answer he wanted, but he got me to ask God, and when God wouldn't give him what he wanted, who else could he blame but the messenger – me?

Anyway, one of Manasseh's other peculiarities was his morbid interest in talking to the dead.[65] Now all Israelites should know that dead people are dead,[66] but Manasseh didn't like that either. His mediums would help him to talk to dead people – and, strangely enough, even the dead always told him what he wanted to hear. I suppose I shouldn't be so sarcastic, but the hopeless folly of those who define their own religion never ceases to amaze and frustrate me. Can't people see through this nonsense? The truth was that Manasseh liked the strange incantations, the chanting, the conjuring tricks, the dressing up in silly clothes, and the lure of freedom from any restraint. How he hated restraint! Even if others applied restraint only to themselves, he found that offensive. I believe this was the source of his hatred of worshippers of Yahweh. He was content enough with people worshipping Yahweh, but only if they would also allow (and never, ever criticise) the worship of other gods. Exclusiveness was intolerable, and obedience to God's commands smacked of exclusiveness in worship.

Any honest Israelite who gave his firstfruits to the temple, or paid a tithe to the Levites, was also "invited" to pay a special tithe to the king. Such special tithes were used for parties. All those who did not pay tithes to the temple were invited to these parties where the 10% given by others was devoured in a gluttonous orgy of lust. If a man paid tithes to the temple a second time, the king's thugs would call and start a street party of a different sort, encouraging neighbours to join in the wanton vandalism of the innocent man's property. Some righteous, and very courageous, men even did this a third time,

---

[65] 2 Kings 21:6

[66] Psalm 6:5; Psalm 146:4; Isaiah 26:19; Psalm 17:15

but they were never seen again after the knock on the door came in the night. Their property was forfeit to the King; their house converted into a shrine for one or other of the lifeless idols which Manasseh worshipped.

What stands out to me as I review the history of that time is something that might not be noticed by most people. To me, however, coming from a priestly family, it is horrific and utterly nauseating: the king was regularly told who had paid tithes or given offerings – told by the priests and Levites serving in the temple. I suppose they felt they had no choice, and that their life would be forfeit if they did anything else; but surely a man must live with himself and with his maker? My family, all of them priests, had survived and even thrived in these times.

King Manasseh had a master plan alright, and his methods gained him a lot of popular support. Many rejoiced that those killjoys who made everyone feel uncomfortable by constantly talking about Yahweh and righteousness were getting their comeuppance at last! Soon the people walked with Manasseh every step of the way.[67]

God had said that the temple in Jerusalem would be a place for his name to live,[68] but Manasseh saw the temple very differently. In his eyes, it was the ideal place for collecting together every possible god he could find to worship.[69] He profaned God's house with a carved image of Asherah.[70] Both of the courts of the house were filled with altars to all the host of heaven[71], and only the priests who could walk the path of compromise lived to tell the tale. The blood of the righteous filled Jerusalem from one end to the other, spilled at the command of the king.[72] Prophets, priests and Levites were favoured targets if they did not rapidly adjust to the new order and speak the words the king wanted to hear.

---

[67] 2 Kings 21:9

[68] 2 Kings 21:7

[69] 2 Kings 21:4-5

[70] 2 Kings 21:7

[71] 2 Kings 21:5, referring to the worship of various celestial objects such as the sun, moon and stars.

[72] 2 Kings 21:16

King Manasseh

My grandfather was High Priest to Yahweh at that time. He survived to a good old age.

Many stories are told about Manasseh, and they are frightening for anyone who worships only Yahweh. True worshippers of Yahweh were his preferred victims, and he bent his inventive talents to finding new ways to kill them. Many say that if Hezekiah had lived much longer, even he would have been in danger from his depraved son. And the story told about the prophet Isaiah when he hid in a tree to escape Manasseh soon after the death of Hezekiah is utterly spine-chilling.

As far as I can tell, no vaguely godly person can find anything good to say about Manasseh for the first fifty years of his reign.

God does not ever abandon his people, so he sent many prophets.[73] Young prophets, old prophets. Prophets from Judah and prophets from desolated Israel. God even sent prophetesses. As far as I can tell from the history books, they all died at the hand of King Manasseh.

And then, suddenly, it happened. Without warning, a rather small army from Assyria marched straight through Israel and arrived at the undefended walls of Jerusalem. Once before, in the time of Hezekiah, the Assyrians had camped outside Jerusalem mouthing threats, but this time there was no faithful king Hezekiah to seek protection from God. Instead, there was Manasseh, fruitlessly offering sacrifices to Baal and Ashtoreth as the commanders of Assyria marched in through the gates of Jerusalem.[74]

It was all very quick. Manasseh was dragged out of the temple he had profaned and his multitude of gods could not protect him. Assyrian brutality was plainly on display as King Manasseh was publicly humiliated, pierced with large fish hooks first through his nose, and then through his lower jaw. Bound in chains of bronze and controlled as necessary by the hooks, he was taken in shame to Babylon.

---

[73] 2 Kings 21:10-15
[74] 2 Chronicles 33:11

Manasseh had got what he deserved – the same sort of suffering that he had brought on so many people more righteous than himself.

But there, in Babylon, he made the first wise decision of his life: he turned to Yahweh.[75]   He prayed and humbled himself completely. In his hour of desperate need, he turned to the one God who could save him; the only god worshipped by anyone who would ever have forgiven him after the boundless contempt that Manasseh had shown for Yahweh. Our God, the God of Israel, is a forgiving God, when there is genuine repentance. No idol worshipped by humans has ever been painted in such forgiving colours. In fact, Yahweh's forgiveness is seen by many as weakness, yet he will by no means clear the guilty. God forgave Manasseh because his repentance was real.

Then, through an amazing series of events, Manasseh was returned to Israel[76] and, breathtakingly, allowed to continue to reign! It is very easy to miss the significance of this miracle. When the Assyrians took Manasseh to Babylon, the kingdom of Judah was over. Finished. Just as the kingdom of Israel had perished about 80 years earlier – and for the same reasons. No-one expected to ever see Manasseh again; indeed, it was surely only a matter of time before the Assyrians returned and carried away many others into captivity. Manasseh's repentance changed all of this. Ah, the glory of God's forgiveness! Yet forgiveness does not always remove punishment, as our great King David found out after his tragic sin in the matter of Bathsheba and Uriah. Yahweh, the judge, forgave Manasseh,[77] but pronounced the certainty of punishment for the entire nation because of the first 50 years of Manasseh's kingship.[78]

There is another small point in this episode that strengthens the faith of all followers of Yahweh. Without Manasseh's repentance, the kingdom of Judah would have come to an ignominious end at the hands of an opportunistic Assyrian invasion; yet God had already prophesied through

---

[75] 2 Chronicles 33:12
[76] 2 Chronicles 33:13
[77] 2 Chronicles 33:19
[78] 2 Kings 23:26 and 24:3-4;

Isaiah that the end would come at the hand of Babylon, not Assyria. Yes: God knew of Manasseh's repentance before ever he led the Assyrians in their lightning raid. What a comfort it is to me to worship Yahweh, the only one who has such foreknowledge.

So Manasseh found himself back on his throne, king once again and free to choose his future. History shows that he kept his promise to God and used his energy and enthusiasm trying to overturn what he had spent 50 years achieving. The last five years of his reign were not recognisable as the work of the same man. Manasseh got rid of the idols from the house of God and threw them outside the city.[79] The altars to other gods were demolished and their rubble thrown outside the city too. God's temple was restored as the centre of worship in Judah[80] – at least to outward appearances.

Yes, Manasseh was genuinely remorseful, but his servants were too steeped in idolatry and lust, too pleased with the power it gave them over people's lives and too corrupt in all they did to really change. The kingdom became a place of two contrasting attitudes: Manasseh wanted his kingdom to reform; his people lusted for more of the sensual pleasures he had promoted in the past. Manasseh wanted the re-consecrated temple to be a pure reflection of a nation turning back to God; the nation wanted nothing to do with purity. Asherah poles and altars to Baal, the sun, the moon and various stars were removed from the temple, and the largest were thrown out into the Kidron Valley. However, many of the smaller items – hundreds, in fact – merely found new homes in people's houses or in quiet corners of the city. Many of the altars and idols in the house of Yahweh were not even removed, but simply hidden in storerooms which the king would never visit. On the face of things, the reforms succeeded – the high places once used for sacrificing to various obscene gods were subsequently only used to offer sacrifices to Yahweh.[81] But in the quieter parts of the city, further from the palace and the eye of the

---

[79] 2 Chronicles 33:15
[80] 2 Chronicles 33:16-17
[81] 2 Chronicles 33:17

reformed king, many roofs became secret centres of worship to the host of heaven. There were no longer public displays of carousing and utter sensual indulgence, but the sensual indulgence continued in private, and waited for the opportunity to throw off all restraint again.

Unfortunately, it is always easier to shout "Stop!" than to make it happen. Not even a king can repent for his people. Sodom and Gomorrah lost only a minor skirmish when Manasseh turned over a new leaf: immorality never gives up. Kings die and reforms die with them, but lust lives on. Every generation shows this truth: lust has many more preachers than self-control does.

Manasseh re-organised the army so that such an embarrassingly easy invasion could not happen again.[82] He put army officers throughout Judah and added an improved communications network to warn of large troop movements or any signs of danger. The walls of Jerusalem were strengthened significantly.

Judah worshipped God again, and it was during this time that my father became old enough to be ordained as a priest. He was present on many occasions as his father – my grandfather, Shallum – taught what he knew of the laws of God to a repentant king. Based on my knowledge now, gleaned from the much older copies of the law found in the reign of Josiah, I feel it was a little like the blind leading the blind. The pens of Manasseh's scribes had taken God's law and made it a lie.[83] I suppose there was enough truth in their writings to help Manasseh a little, but the lies they mixed with that truth remained unchallenged for another quarter of a century, putting the final nails in the coffin of the kingdom of Judah. Manasseh reaped what he had sown: he had only allowed dishonest scribes to copy God's laws in his early years, and so their twisted writings were the only knowledge of God available to him when what he really wanted was the truth.

---

[82] 2 Chronicles 33:14
[83] Hints are found in Jeremiah 8:8.

King Manasseh

I was but two years old when Manasseh died, so I have no memory of his repentance, nor any memory of the work of Amon, his successor in evil whose reign lasted a brief but evil two years. Manasseh's wife – Amon's mother – was no faithful woman such as might have been chosen by Hezekiah had he lived to do so. No, Meshullemeth was a true daughter of Haruz of Jotbah, famous as an obsequious supporter of Manasseh at his worst, and her son Amon immediately busied himself with the process of reversing Manasseh's reforms, recovering the idols and altars from the Kidron Valley and reinstating them in the house of God.[84] Fortunately for the nation, his servants conspired against him and killed him. However, by that time, he had already re-established the altars and idols in the house of God, along with all of the hateful practices that went with them.

Judah was at an all-time low. The lifestyle of God's people was worse than that of the Amorites whom God had driven out of the land to give it to Israel. The land had vomited out the Amorites[85] and the Israelites, and was preparing to vomit out Judah too.[86]

---

[84] 2 Chronicles 33:22
[85] Leviticus 18:25
[86] Leviticus 18:28

CR

Postscript:

If you feel that this description exaggerates Manasseh's evil, maybe you could consider another couple of facts about his degenerate behaviour that I have not yet mentioned:

- Manasseh "caused his son to pass through the fire"[87] – a fine-sounding euphemism meaning that, although God had given him a son, Manasseh burned him to death as an offering to a dead idol.[88]

- God commanded Israel never to seek out wizards and assigned the death penalty as the punishment;[89] Manasseh sought out wizards and magicians often.[90]

Yes, Manasseh was worse than any of the kings of Judah or Israel before him, and worse even than the kings of the Amorites whom God drove out of the land before his people. His lifestyle had first copied[91] and then further developed the ways of the Amorites and the Canaanites.[92] Manasseh had charted a course for the nation that could never be reversed.

What a tragic result of God's gift to Hezekiah of fifteen extra years.

---

[87] 2 Kings 21:6
[88] Ezekiel 16:20-21
[89] Leviticus 19:31; Leviticus 20:6, 27
[90] 2 Kings 21:6
[91] 2 Chronicles 33:1-7
[92] 2 Chronicles 33:9

Chapter 8

Day Two

Once again, the morning meal was a time of confrontation in our home. After the blessing of the food, I got in first by announcing: "I must go to Jerusalem again today to continue warning the people about God's plans."

"But what about your lessons?" asked my father. "Immer, your teacher, was asking me yesterday where you were. He was not much pleased when I told him that you were wandering around the markets and gates of Jerusalem warning of imminent punishment and destruction. Really, my son, you are too young to be lecturing us all. The elders of our people have been managing the delicate balances of life for much longer than you. We know how to walk the path of righteousness and tolerance; we know when to stand straight and when to bend with the wind. We worship Yahweh our God. He will be pleased with that, and so should you be."

Azariah took his turn next: "A young upstart like you lecturing even the people who advise King Josiah. What a cheek!"

"What do you mean?" I asked, a little puzzled by this accusation.

"Didn't you see Achbor, Shaphan, Ahikam and the others yesterday? I believe that they went and listened to each of your ill-advised harangues, and that you completely ignored them. You should learn to show a little respect to the king's nobles." Azariah was putting junior in his place again.

So that was who the well-dressed men were! A small thrill of excitement ran through me – maybe I had achieved more yesterday than I knew. Maybe these men would listen to God's message and the kingdom could be saved. They were very important men in Judah: I knew their names, of course, but I did not know them by sight – they didn't tend to associate with young students.

As I considered this, Gemariah joined in, more thoughtful as usual, but still critical: "Josiah has made good choices in serving Yahweh and is leading the people well. Your message seems to suggest that he and his kingdom are all evil. It doesn't seem fair."

I couldn't completely disagree with Gemariah, then. Josiah was a wonderful king. He led the people in godliness and set a magnificent example, yet it seemed that God's words had already condemned the entire kingdom to inevitable destruction. At that time, it was hard to fully understand the situation and the contradiction that seemed to exist. Looking back, I'm still not sure how much of a change Josiah or even David could ever have achieved with our nation. Maybe an immediate repentance like that of the people of Nineveh would have altered the result; there's no way to know now.

Mother worked on in the background as usual, and the troubled look on her face made me feel guilty. I was the one who was causing all this trouble.

I did my best to answer Gemariah: "Gemariah, the king worships God with all his heart and wants us all to do the same, but you don't need to go far outside Jerusalem to see the idols everywhere, the high places and altars to the stars, and the tragic grave markers for all the little children callously murdered for Molech. Josiah's reforms don't seem to be having any impact on those abuses, and the people who revel in them form the majority of our nation. God's words are very clear. We need to try to understand them, not just reject them because they aren't what we expect."

"Young man," my father was pontificating again, "we are blessed with a knowledge of the love of the God who led our nation out of its captivity in Egypt. Yet he urges us to be wise; to live in harmony with each other. Certainly King Josiah encourages us to worship Yahweh, but kings come and kings go – his father was not so single-minded, and who knows what the next king will be like? Our great king Solomon showed us how to worship God wisely, without unduly upsetting those who have not yet learned the ways of God. God blessed Solomon with riches and fame because of his wisdom in this. He was a man of peace. Remember the words of the Preacher: 'Do not be overly righteous'.[93] You will wear yourself out with so-called righteousness if you can't get the balance right. Things are not always as black and white as you were suggesting yesterday."

I had heard much of this before, but now I was re-evaluating it in the face of God's expressed opinion of his people:

"you defiled my land and made my heritage an abomination"[94]

and

"as many as your cities are your gods".[95]

I really must find the time to read the scrolls that could be trusted to contain the word of God. As far as I could remember, there were many places in our scriptures where God encouraged exactly the opposite of tolerance: worship of other gods was to be treated with as much tolerance as one might show to a snake biting a child! In fact, the summaries of the later years of Solomon didn't praise him for wisdom, but lamented the fact that he was led away from God to the pagan worship of the gods of his many wives. My father and my teachers had tended to gloss over these things and concentrate

---

[93] Ecclesiastes 7:16

[94] Jeremiah 2:7

[95] Jeremiah 2:28

on Solomon's wonderful wisdom, but hadn't our nation been split into two kingdoms because of Solomon's unfaithfulness?

"Anyway, Father," I said, "I have a job to do and I must do it. The word of Yahweh must be obeyed." I heard myself say the words, but it seemed a little unreal. For me to speak to my father in such a way was unheard of; I had never done it before. Categoric, non-negotiable and blunt – like an iron pillar or bronze walls. That was what God had said, and now he was making it happen. His words to me I could still read in glowing letters in my mind: "…against the kings of Judah, its officials, its priests[96]" – where would this all end? I was no wise elder whom everybody would expect to speak in this way when necessary. Rather, I was a seventeen-year-old youngest child who was yet to finish his schooling, and I feared the repercussions. But for the moment, it worked! The young upstart spoke so to God's High Priest and overcame. Apart from a few grumbles, my father accepted that I would no longer attend school, but would speak the word of God to the people. I wonder whether he ever accepted that it really was the word of God?

☙

Gemariah walked with me to Jerusalem that morning. He was always the one of my family who was closest to seeing God's truth, and I still miss him. If only he could have made the leap of faith that Ebed-Melech made… but he could never quite accept that you can't walk with God and still walk with the majority. If only I could have been more convincing that morning.

Wending our way up the paths toward Har Hatsophim, the warmth of the sun was fighting the chill of the fitful breeze. It was good to have his companionship as we walked and talked that sunlit morn. For the time being, I was content to have any support I could get to help me understand my new work. He asked what had happened when God spoke to me and how it had felt. He asked me whether God had said why he would

---

[96] Jeremiah 1:18

speak to me and not to my father, or even directly to King Josiah. He asked if I was sure it really was the word of God. And he asked me whether God's sentence of destruction would really happen, or would it be conditional on our response – as with Jonah's message to Nineveh – or could it even be hyperbole (if it was right to suggest such a thing of God's word). I could not answer this last question at the time, and I suppose it doesn't really matter anymore, but it did then. History shows what happened: exactly what God had said from the start. So often, conjecture and philosophising can distract us from God's immediate message, and the opportunity is missed. If only Gemariah's questions that day could have concentrated on "what can I do to change God's judgement?" – but only a handful of my fellow Israelites ever responded like that, and the judgement did not change.

That morning walk to Jerusalem had the beginnings of the awkwardness that would steadily grow between us. It was probably the last time Gemariah and I walked together in the companionship of two brothers who were good friends. God's word would gradually tear us apart.

Chapter 9

Judah's Nobles

I was repeating God's word for the third time that day when the six mysterious men arrived. A chill wind had risen and it was becoming more difficult to make myself heard as I stood in the open space before the gates of the temple of God. Eddies of brittle leaves swirled and scraped over the pavement; noisily flapping canopies hid merchants carefully wrapping their mantles more closely around them; beggars sporadically shouted their entreaties, but the exercise could not restore warmth to their filthy limbs. As usual, I had found an elevated place to speak from – the front of a cart delivering woollen fleeces and dye to the temple. The driver was unloading the fleeces as I warned the people about their neglect of God and his inexorable judgement that was marching ever closer.

And that was when I saw them: elegantly attired and impeccably presented, with neatly trimmed moustaches and tidy beards. Once again, the crowd opened up respectfully in front of them until they chose a place where they could easily hear my words. Again they listened without any obvious response. But this time when I finished, they moved in my direction. Their leader was a man who exuded confidence and assurance. He was obviously used to shaping events as he chose and he walked towards me purposefully. The others accompanied him, as if they had all agreed beforehand what they should do. His eyes were striking; when he looked at you he gave the impression that he could see inside you and read your thoughts.

"I am Maaseiah," he greeted me. "I work for King Josiah in the administration of this magnificent city."[97] His voice was pleasing and a smile lifted the corners of his mouth and softened his sharp features. "You are very young for such a serious message. Young Asaiah here is not very pleased with what you were saying. He is very loyal to King Josiah and doesn't like any criticism of him – even implied criticism – and you *are* criticising a king when you criticise his kingdom."

"Yahweh of armies gave me the words to speak," I objected, "and when God speaks a word, I must pass it on."

You may be thinking that I was a rather arrogant young man, always quick with an aggressive rejoinder, but I had never considered myself to be at all like that before the word of the Lord came to me. On the contrary, I was a rather quiet young man, ready to listen to others and slow to defend myself against criticism. All that seemed to have changed with the voice of God and his promise to provide an iron resistance within me as long as I would not allow myself to be frightened by my critics. It was hard to get used to and didn't always feel right.

Maaseiah's face was impassive and he seemed to be withholding judgement until he had more evidence – or maybe more indication of the mood of the majority. However, Asaiah's dark face showed clearly his displeasure at my message: "How dare you speak of my lord Josiah's kingdom in that way? How dare you suggest that God could be anything other than happy with how the kingdom is returning to him? Josiah is a wonderful man, a magnificent king and the best worshipper of God. There has never been a king like him in all

---

[97] By the eighteenth year of Josiah, Maaseiah was the governor of Jerusalem (2 Chronicles 34:8).

Judah who has turned to God with all his heart – and yet you say that Judah will be destroyed for turning away from God! Foolishness! I don't know who you are, but it is clear that you are no prophet of God and no friend of the king. The Lord did not send you!" Asaiah spoke forcefully and the look in his eyes suggested that he would be happy to join a stoning mob with me as the prime target. It shocked me deeply: I loved Josiah as a righteous king and a dedicated shepherd of God's people, yet here was a man who would happily kill me for criticising the king, whom I had no desire or intention to criticise at all!

"I don't mean to criticise our king," I stammered.

"Then you should stop saying that his kingdom is evil and will be destroyed," said Asaiah. "My lord Josiah's life's work is to rule this nation. If you say the nation is no good, you are saying Josiah is no good. And you are wrong! People like you should be stoned." He spat on the ground in front of me. I was horrified: a close friend of the king wanted to kill me! This was not what I had expected, even in my worst nightmares. I could feel fear building up in me, but I forced it down.

"Was Moses no good?" I replied, as calmly as I could. "God described Israel as bad many times while Moses was their leader, but that did not make Moses bad, or even a bad leader." Maybe I was just naïve – in fact I probably was – but it hadn't occurred to me that criticising the nation would be taken as a criticism of its king. I was certain that Josiah was not the main target of God's word. It was others who were not serving God. It was others who kept the shrines of Baal, Asherah, Chemosh and all the host of heaven busy in the back streets of the town. They and their false prophets. Yet Asaiah's response to God's message was nothing but hatred for the messenger. But… *was* God also criticising Josiah, as Asaiah averred? No time to think about it now, but I must do so later.

"Asaiah, you young hothead," said a third man, one I faintly recognised now that I could see him up close, "tone down your baying for blood. Manasseh is not our lord anymore." There was a disarming smile on his lips, but a hint of serious warning as well.

I had seen him before, but could not quite place him. Fortunately he introduced himself and saved me the difficulty of working out whether I should know his name or not.

"I am Shaphan," he announced, "King Josiah's secretary. Young Asaiah here often wants to solve problems by stoning people or taking off their heads. He is too young to realise how terrible a kingdom is which follows that path. I knew too many good men who were slaughtered in the streets of Jerusalem – and taking vengeance just adds to the problem."

So this was Shaphan, newly appointed secretary to King Josiah – and an increasingly close friend of my father's, although I had never met him personally. I had seen him briefly last year when Josiah had announced to the crowd his plans to cleanse Jerusalem of all the high places and the images which had still adorned many houses and open places in the city. Shaphan had stood on the platform with King Josiah and passed him the scroll from which he had read his proclamation. He was known as a godly man, loyal and true – just the sort of man Josiah wanted by his side. I too would be very grateful for his loyalty and that of his family in later years.

"Anyway, we wanted to talk to you about your message," he continued. "We have heard it several times now, and feel that we understand the thrust of your message. You are the son of a priest to be sure, but can you tell us on what authority you are making these announcements?"

"Yes, I am Jeremiah," I said, "the son of Hilkiah, one of the priests of Anathoth in the land of Benjamin. The word of Yahweh came to me in the night, just two nights ago. He gave me no sign or miracle to prove I am his messenger. All he gave me was his word, a command that I should not worry about being too young to do the work, and a promise that he would be with me as long as I obeyed."

" 'One of the priests' – shouldn't you say the High Priest?" Shaphan's question was put with a wry smile. "Is that humility on your part, young man, or are you belittling your father's position? Some of your words have suggested that you don't have a high opinion of our priests."

"My lord secretary, you have not heard my opinions," I replied, "only God's. Yahweh's feelings in Yahweh's words."

"Can you tell me your own feelings now, then?"

"At the moment, I am still trying to understand what God's words tell me of his feelings. He is so great that it is difficult. It's a struggle I am probably only just beginning," I said ruefully.

"Be careful, or your words may cost you your family, young Jeremiah." Shaphan's words were spoken thoughtfully; how prophetic they turned out to be. "However," he continued, "the question is, can we be sure of your loyalty to king Josiah?"

The question gave me pause. Was I loyal to king Josiah? Another matter I had not thought about – another conflict of interests.

Now that I was a prophet of God, Yahweh obviously had first call on my loyalty. Yet I was also finding it terribly hard to tell whom he approved of and whom he hated. Oh, the evil extremes were easy to recognise, but on the side with an appearance of good, there seemed to be much more complexity. Those categories of people who appeared good to me had been the targets of God's criticism too. I had to choose my words carefully, but had to be honest too. "My first loyalty is to Yahweh. While we have a king who follows God's law, he can be sure of my complete loyalty." It was true, and it was all I could say. If Josiah served God, I would serve and obey him. But was God satisfied with King Josiah? In promising to keep me strong in the face of opposition, his words had been, "against the whole land, *against the kings of Judah....*" What a terrifying thought – having to stand against Josiah, my childhood hero. Was this commitment to include Josiah, or just some other, later kings of Judah? I wasn't sure, and knew that here was even more that I would need to pray about. I needed to find the time urgently, but Shaphan was continuing.

"Come now, Jeremiah, we need a strong commitment, not mealy-mouthed half-promises." Shaphan's eyes were also rather striking, like Maaseiah's. When he looked at you, he really looked at you, and his speech challenged everyone who listened to him. He seemed to expect the best that people could offer, and mostly they would give it. But I was forced to disappoint him.

"My lord Shaphan," I replied quietly, "what more can I say? You must judge for yourself whether you have a right to demand my unquestioning loyalty to Josiah, but I have no choice: I can only give my unqualified loyalty to Yahweh."

"Your statements are fine and high sounding," Shaphan's voice had a harsh edge to it now, "but how can we fill an army, God's army, if each citizen maintains the right of veto and all of the king's subjects decide their loyalty anew every day?" He looked at me again with his chin slightly raised and a challenging look in his eyes.

"If Josiah maintains his loyalty to God, he won't need to worry about armies – Yahweh of armies will take care of the kingdom," I replied, with youthful certainty.

"To be sure, Yahweh will judge Josiah's loyalty, but you sound as if you want that job yourself, young man." Sardonic this time – while a slightly crooked smile played around the edges of his mouth.

"You asked me to guarantee my loyalty," I said, "but all I can say is that my loyalty is to Yahweh first. I am not against the king – I have admired him all my life. But Yahweh is my God, a God above all kings, and he is the one who called me to be a prophet."

"And that was just two nights ago?" A mere artifice this, intended to poke fun at how little experience I had at this job.

"Yes, my lord."

Shaphan swung his robe around him with a little gesture of disdain. "Not long to ponder on his words – or even to make sure you have got them right!" Obviously the words had upset Shaphan. I wondered which words had hurt most.

"Oh, I know that I have got them right," I replied. "There is no doubt about that at all. Yahweh put his words in my mouth, and they still burn within me like a fire. There is no possibility of mixing them up." The words were glowing again inside my mind as I spoke. Burning. Fighting to escape my control and pour out again on God's people who were gathering now to hear the discussion. I looked up at the sky, a vast pale blue bowl with a few nebulous white clouds hurrying, shapeless in the weak sunlight, and felt again the wonder of hearing the voice of God and seeing the clouds he had sculpted. The Word was burning, hot and bright, and it was with difficulty that I swallowed it down and looked away from the sky.

Shaphan was one of the most perceptive men I have ever known, and he must have seen the fight within me, for he said abruptly, "I mustn't keep you any longer, but I have just one more question: In what way have the shepherds of Judah sinned against Yahweh?[98] What have we done, that we should be condemned by you?"

There it was again: "condemned by *you*". Would no-one ever believe that these were the words of God? I was condemning no-one; God was condemning everyone. Maybe I wasn't making it clear enough that these words were not mine. I would try again. "God says the shepherds have been transgressing ever since Israel entered this land and will still be doing so when our grandchildren are taking over the reins. His repeated complaint is our lack of loyalty to him. Other nations stick to their gods, even though they are dead idols with empty heads, but Israel has turned away from the only true and living God, even though he has proved his power beyond question so many times. Throughout these centuries, the shepherds have not stopped this faithlessness in his people, although that is their most important work."

Another of the six, a younger man – like Asaiah, he looked about the same age as King Josiah – spoke up: "You see, father, I told you it was just a general criticism, referring mostly to people who are long dead. Just think of the times of the judges and of those evil kings who abandoned the God of our fathers. It's not hard to see that you and the others shepherding our people now are infinitely better than, say, Athaliah and her minions."

---

[98] Jeremiah 2:8

His words gave me the clue I needed to put a name to him. This must be Ahikam, the son of Shaphan, a rising star in the leadership of Judah: young, ambitious and very bright. I was later to learn that he was also a loyal and godly friend, but one who would always be plagued by his attachment to his position of influence. How hard it is for people who have tasted a position of power and then must choose between God and power. I believe that Ahikam honestly tried to be loyal to Yahweh – but he too is dead now, and discussing his final choices cannot help him. God is our judge.

Ahikam was wearing the clothes you might expect of a young nobleman, with a finely woven outer garment made in the colourful checked style imported from the Phoenicians of Tyre and Sidon. It was wrapped closely around him to keep out the biting wind of that cold, clear day. His sandals seemed to be a new style also, with the toes completely enclosed in leather, and I wished my own feet were similarly protected from the wind's icy fingers. Maybe I could get some of this new footwear, particularly if God's work was going to keep me outdoors for hours as the blustery afternoon cooled into a frigid evening. It didn't seem right to ask where he had got them – should a prophet of God discuss the latest fashions in footwear? I wasn't sure of the answer, so I let it pass. What I could not let pass was Ahikam's assumption that God's criticism of Judah applied to everyone else but us. I had heard this attitude several times as I had spoken God's message: some said it referred to the northern kingdom, some said it referred to past leaders or those who lived in other cities of Judah, but no-one seemed to want to take God's words for themselves!

"My lord Ahikam," I said, "These words were not sent to those who are dead or to those who live a long way away: they are sent to the people of Jerusalem, to leaders and led, to rich and poor, to young and old; kings, rulers, priests and people. The punishment is coming on all because all have sinned against God. Here at the entrance to God's temple we must think about his holiness and repent of our sins. The message is for you. God said:

" 'You have *all* transgressed against me.'[99] "

Ahikam's eyebrows rose and the smile faded from his face. He turned towards me and spoke seriously: "Isn't Josiah better than Athaliah? Aren't the nobles Josiah has chosen better than Manasseh's thugs? Aren't we innocent by comparison? Hasn't God's anger turned from Judah since Josiah became king?"

It was such a temptation to just agree and get on with speaking to the crowd, but… *"an iron pillar, and bronze walls"*? I must make the stand: "Yahweh is trying to tell us that he wants holiness from us, not comparisons. Don't compare Judah with Israel; compare us with God's angels. Don't compare Josiah with Athaliah; compare him with Moses or David. Don't compare yourself with past nobles but with Samuel or Elijah. Judah has become degenerate and God's judgement is coming."

Ahikam looked at Shaphan and Shaphan looked at Ahikam. They weren't pleased, but they didn't continue to argue. Asaiah had continued to look at me with a smouldering dislike that tended towards hatred, and his lip curled when he saw me looking at him. I wasn't going to convince him! As we had talked, Maaseiah and the remaining two members of the group of six had edged over to one side, where a merchant's canopy offered a limited protection from the cold, and stood there talking. Ahikam called to them, "Maaseiah, Achbor, Micri: we have learned what we need. Now we must tell Josiah about young Jeremiah and his message."

The three strode across to where we stood: "So is he genuine?" asked the taller of the two whose names I still did not know. "Is he speaking from God as he claims?"

"I don't know, Achbor," said Shaphan; "only time will tell."

Again the squally wind wrapped me in its bitter embrace, and I longed for the benevolent warmth of a comfortable fire burning on our family hearth. Oh, for its soothing heat to drive away the numbing cold that had spread through my bones as

---

[99] Jeremiah 2:29

we talked near the gate of God's house. Despite the failure of the late rains, winter was receding slowly, reluctantly.

The six walked away. Their fine clothes were flapping in the wind, and I was sure that those new closed-in sandals must have been keeping their noble feet much warmer than mine. I shivered as I watched them stride out of sight around the corner towards the palace. I wondered what they would report to King Josiah. How would the king respond to their news? Was I right to keep hammering this negative message? Shaphan was right: in criticising the kingdom, I was criticising the king… but it was God's word; I had no choice but to tell it – did I?

&

All of the fleeces and dye had been unloaded from the wagon and it was rumbling away as I looked for another place from which to broadcast the message. The irony of delivering God's message of condemnation from that particular cart did not become obvious to me until several years later. I continued my work standing on a low wall. I was finding all too quickly that being a prophet was hard and lonely work – and cold!

Chapter 10

Reflection

That evening I walked back toward Anathoth alone in the gathering gloom. The sky was clear and swallows darted here and there: a distant silhouette one moment, an unexpected dark shape speeding across my path the next. Stars were appearing in the dark indigo expanse and twinkling coldly. A gusty wind made the evening feel more like the depths of winter than the start of spring. But the sky was clear and the heavens were showing the glory of the creator. And I felt again the paradox that is at the heart of our interactions with God: God fills the universe and is always close; yet mostly we cannot see, touch or hear him any more than we can touch the stars. I walked slowly, as I had much to think about, while the evening sank into an icy night. I knew the path so well that I was not concerned with getting lost or injured; what I desperately needed was some answers from God.

Was God criticising – even condemning – Josiah in the words he had given me to speak? If God were to write his current assessment of Josiah, would it be like his judgement of David the son of Jesse, or more like his judgement of Jeroboam the son of Nebat? Like Jehoshaphat or Saul? I thought of the words of Asaiah: "There has never been a king like him in all Judah who has turned to God with all his heart." Was it true? He had begun his reign as an eight-year-old – a young lad put on the throne at the insistence of the people of the land after the assassination of his father Amon. The son of the house of David must still be king, and the assassins were immediately executed.

What else could an eight-year-old ruler be but a puppet? Those who pulled the strings were content to rule the land while presenting Josiah as the figurehead. No authority; no leadership; no initiative; just a title and a sweet young face – such were the nobles' expectations of Josiah. But the young king showed that he had a will of his own a little earlier than anyone expected. When he was still little more than a boy – just 16 years old – he made a complete break with his father's religious ideas. He wanted to worship Yahweh, and he searched and researched to find out how he should do that. In truth, few could tell him, but many were willing to try.

Over the next four years, Josiah determinedly sifted out the truth from the jumble of religious twaddle he was fed. Slowly, he gathered around him friends and advisors who would not completely reject his growing faith but would instead provide wise guidance. By the twelfth year of his reign, he was sure enough of his faith to start a purge. Just after his twentieth birthday he made the big announcement: idols were to be completely removed from his kingdom. Baal, Asherah, Molech, Milcom, Tammuz and all the host of heaven were to go. Cast or carved, glazed or painted, metal, clay, wood or straw; all idols must be destroyed. The outcry was enormous. Unfortunately, in Judah the organised worship of Yahweh was not so easy to separate from the worship of a multitude of other gods. Most people found little difficulty in worshipping Yahweh as well as Molech or Baal or Milcom. Legends told of the amazing work of Yahweh in bringing Israel out of Egypt, but it would be foolish, most said, to omit the worship of Baal when it could be improving your business success and general good fortune. The demands of some gods were more difficult to satisfy, but many parents were willing to sacrifice a son to improve the chances of success for their other children. A brutal superstition.

But Josiah understood enough of Yahweh to see that this could never satisfy him; Yahweh was an exclusive god. According to Yahweh, worship of any other god – be it one, or twenty or a thousand – was utterly unacceptable. Brutal superstition cannot mix with a pure faith. Josiah perceived that any worship of another god made genuine worship of Yahweh impossible. Josiah recognised what so few kings before him had ever recognised (and, sadly, none of the kings after him ever saw), namely that worshipping Yahweh required a complete separation from any other worship at all. This was a world-defying discovery, and enforcing exclusive worship in his kingdom was never going to be easy. His advisers whined and cajoled. The old men stroked their beards and shook their heads. The young men tried to convince him to try a bit of luxurious royal living for a while before he constrained himself – and everyone else – in such draconian fashion. Various important women sent delegations to seek exemptions for "cultural activities". Priests of the newly illegal foreign gods raised all sorts of objections and spoke urgently to anyone in the palace who they hoped might be able to drop a convincing word in the young king's ear.

Josiah overrode them all. The high places, where a free and easy populace worshipped all sorts of gods in all sorts of ways, were shut down. Josiah desecrated them, painted out the religious signs and symbols, hounded the priests to find more useful employment, and knocked down altars and sacred buildings. He personally supervised the removal work and often turned the high places into toilets. The people cheered and sang, but kept worshipping at other high places all the same. Josiah widened the net and ordered his men to cut down every altar to Baal in all of Jerusalem. But nothing happened. Of course, there were always reasons why. The weather was bad; the workers didn't turn up for work, or forgot to bring their tools; the supervisors got their orders mixed up and went to a different place from where the labourers went; the workers had accidents and had to stop work almost before they had started; or the altars weren't there when they arrived (although they had mysteriously reappeared by the next day when they were surrounded by worshippers at early dawn).

How can a king enforce his will on an unwilling populace? He could have followed the path of his grandfather and filled the streets with blood. He could have given in and let everyone do what was right in his own eyes. He could have tried to bribe the people by adding their favourite forms of worship to the worship of Yahweh – but that was no different from the existing situation anyway. Instead, he persisted and carefully tried some different methods to achieve his reforms.

Josiah started to personally attend each of the events he had ordered each day. Altars to Baal were cut down in his presence, and no supervisor dared to get the orders mixed up then. Labourers turned up in the right place at the right time to obey the king's orders. And while the threat of punishment was not made openly, it was felt by the pagan priests as they watched the bones of long-dead priests being burned on the ruins of their altars. Everyone agreed that Josiah was a kind and gentle young man, but he always seemed to do what he believed in and no-one dared to openly flout his commands. Who wanted to be the first to be burned on an altar to Baal just to desecrate it?

So Josiah's purge progressed, but the people were not wholly with him. If Josiah was not present when high places were to be removed, the work was still not completed. Mostly, it never started, so Josiah tried to make sure that he was always there – early. A king can overlook a lack of cooperation up to a point, but if it is seen to happen too often, the ugly picture of rebellion is painted in the streets. Josiah was too wise to let that happen.

The signs were all there that Josiah was genuine and that his commitment towards Yahweh was still developing. So why had God given me the words to speak which I had been speaking?

Could it be possible that Josiah was not genuinely worshipping God? No, I could not believe that. Well, maybe he was not trying hard enough to stop the false worship. But I couldn't really believe that either. It seemed to me that he was achieving more than any other king had ever achieved. And yet it seemed that even this was not enough. Judah was to be destroyed despite the tireless work of Josiah. But how could that be true? Judah was Yahweh's people. We were all sons of Abraham. We were Israelites indeed. I could personally trace my ancestry back to Abraham, and knew that I was an heir to the promises God had made him.

As I mused on these things, the obvious answer suddenly came to me: the nation really had become too bad for Josiah to fix. There was no remedy to Manasseh's evil and the evil of a cooperating nation. So was Josiah simply wasting his time? Should he simply follow the advice of some of his younger friends and eat, drink and be merry? Should he enjoy the good life while the nation tottered and stumbled inevitably towards destruction? Is that what God's message meant for Judah?

By this time, it was completely dark, and I had stopped at a dip in the path where it crossed a gully. At this time of year, water normally flowed across the path, dropping from a flat rock that jutted out from the hillside just above the path. This year was no ordinary year, and no water was flowing. I stepped up onto the rock, then sat and digested this latest idea. Some thin clouds were now scudding across the sky and the stars were briefly hidden from time to time. Being early in the month, there was still only a thin sliver of moon which had almost dropped to the horizon, and the flickering of the stars seemed colder than before. The vast expanse of heaven had not changed, but I was finding it less welcoming than it had been just a few minutes before.

Had God made Josiah and placed him over Judah as king to do a job which could never be successful? Would Judah inevitably be destroyed, however well Josiah ruled? The words of Isaiah came into my head: "How long O Lord?"[100], with the terrible answer of God: "Until cities lie waste without inhabitant."[101] But wait, the cities of Judah were still not lying waste without inhabitant – why? Could it be that the answer lay in the work of a good king – Hezekiah? God's answer to

---

[100] Isaiah 6:11
[101] Isaiah 6:11

Isaiah had assumed no change to the nation, but Hezekiah had inspired a change. Would my message be the same? Categorically catastrophic, but open to change if the nation repented and changed? Surely it must be that way, or Josiah's godly approach to his job could never achieve anything. I thought about this as the moon set, turning all the possibilities over in my mind while nothing was left in the sky but the brightness of the stars and the few flitting clouds.

And then I prayed. Finally, I prayed. I prayed for understanding, and I prayed for forgiveness for my nation. I begged God to accept the righteous devotion of Josiah my king and to forgive the sin of my people. And I wondered what I could do to help. Prayer can be a difficult, exhausting business at times. Impersonal prayer is easy, and formal prayer can be almost a technical exercise, but intimate prayer communing with Yahweh as a jealous God is utterly draining, and feels almost unreasonable. To ask God to wipe away sin and grant forgiveness when I know that his judgement is just… how could I justify this? Yet Moses did precisely this, and God forgave, so how could I leave the prayers unuttered?

Father, please forgive me and my people.

The night grew colder still and my reverie continued. I knew that I should be returning home and that my family might be worried about me; but the needs of a nation seemed greater, and the need to understand more urgent.

I wondered whether the disaster was as imminent as that about which Jonah had warned Nineveh – the disaster which never happened because of the astonishing repentance of an entire city of pagans. Was it possible that in forty days God would destroy Jerusalem? Logic suggested that since God had made the deadline clear to Nineveh, he would have done the same to Jerusalem if such an immediate deadline existed: but what about the flood in Noah's time? I had no real idea of how long it would be before the axe would fall on Jerusalem and Judah.

Overall, I felt that I had gained some understanding of how God was working and why my message offered no way out for the nation. But I felt also that for God to have announced the message in that way must mean that the possibility of modification, forgiveness, atonement or restitution was very small, and very strongly connected with Josiah's reforming zeal. Possibly the only hope for Judah was in an immediate and positive response to Josiah's call for acceptance of Yahweh as the only God of Judah, and God's message through me was given to help stir the nation's heart at the last possible moment.

And I could already tell that it was not working. Josiah's cleansing of Jerusalem was not gaining a heartfelt response of honour to God. He could get short term cooperation, lip service really, but no heartfelt response of repentance. My own words had gained an initial emotional response, but the response had faded when the audience had realised that they could easily apply the words to someone other than themselves – to Israel, to past kings, to evil priests. No-one had fallen down on the ground in utter horror at the enumerated sins of Judah. No-one had torn his clothes and cried out for forgiveness. No ashes had been thrown in the air, there was just an immediate return to trading and "ordinary" life, once the sideshow finished. Was there any way to make Judah realise that what they thought of as a sideshow was the real material of life?

How could the people be moved to turn once again? Josiah yearned for such a response and so did I – but it wasn't coming. Was there any way I could help to trigger it? What could trigger the recognition that their response now was the most utterly urgent thing that would happen in their entire lifetime?

Father, forgive? Father, turn your people's heart back to you again?

Chapter 11

Trying Harder

Seeing the lights of torches weaving down the trail towards me, I slipped off my rock of reverie and stumbled towards them in the starlight. It was my father and Azariah. They were worried and angry; concerned but irate. The night air was frigid, and seemed to crackle in my throat as I called out, "Shalom. The Lord be with you."

"Jeremiah!" my father cried, "The Lord keep you." The answer seemed to catch in his throat also as we hurried towards each other.

As my father embraced me, it suddenly occurred to me that he must have been worried. I had been so taken up with my own thoughts and worries that I had given no thought to others; no thought to the dangers of the night; no thought to food, or my mother's gentle concern.

"I'm sorry, Father," I said meekly, "I was lost in my thoughts and didn't notice how late it was getting."

"Never mind," was his curt reply. "Let's get you back home and then we can talk."

Azariah made no comment, but I sensed the mixed feelings of relief at finding the lost, and irritation at my thoughtlessness.

We climbed the path to Anathoth together, making our way towards the familiar shape of our house, a black outline against the moonless, cloudless sky. A welcoming shaft of light crept under the door, but there was none of the delicious smell of cooking that normally greeted me on my return from Jerusalem. A brief pang of regret struck me – my mother's hot stew was something to long for – but it quickly passed as I felt again the value of this time of self-examination and growing recognition of God.

My thoughts had been leading me to despair, but gradually, under the impassive light of the stars, the comfort of God had come through my gloomy reverie, and the encouragement to keep trying. The lights from the heavens seemed more personal again, and I felt that I could keep going. Even the valley of the shadow of death could be walked without fear, as long as God was with me. So, tomorrow, I would try even harder to get God's message across.

Someone would listen. God wouldn't send me on a completely meaningless mission – would he? There was still a sneaking doubt as I envisaged a nation in which no-one would listen, but to whom God continued to send messengers. Maybe Noah had felt like that as he explained why he was building the ark. Never mind. I would continue, but first I would need to face the consequences of my hours of absence.

Leading the way, my father opened the door. Inside, I saw my mother sitting, tense and alone, worried lines etched across her face. I felt guilty. As she saw me, relief lit up her face, and with a flash of God-given insight, I realised how hard it would be to serve both God and family. Could I have done things differently that night? How could I ever have found the uninterrupted hours I needed, without taking the opportunity I took? At home, I would have been busy: chores, discussions, arguments and plans would have devoured every minute, and my time with God would never have arrived. Being inside our house meant being surrounded by distractions. Outside, alone in the dark; that was the only place I could possibly commune with God and begin to understand his work. Was explanation possible? With regret I decided that it wasn't, and forced myself to walk in as if nothing unusual had happened.

"We found him down by the flat rock," my father explained to my mother. "He tells us he was 'thinking'."

"Jeremiah, are you alright?" my mother asked. Concern tinged her voice as she hurried across the room and laid her hand on my arm.

"I'm fine, mother. Sorry not to have let you know I wasn't coming."

"We thought you must have stayed in Jerusalem for dinner. Immer, your teacher, saw you talking to the nobles at the gate of the temple and suggested you might be having a meal with them to explain your new work. But when you didn't come after dinner, we started to get worried. You've never done anything like this to us before." Disappointment was mixed with the worry in my mother's voice.

Maybe I should try to explain anyway. "I was trying to understand how God feels about Josiah," I said slowly, "and why he has sent a message of complete condemnation when Josiah seems to be a righteous man. I wanted to understand."

"Did you find your answers?" my mother asked.

"How can you find any answers, sitting on a damp rock in the pitch black of a freezing night?" interrupted my father. Azariah laughed.

"Yes," I said simply, "I think I did."

It was very late; all the servants had already left, and we went to bed soon after that. I suppose that I appreciated the care that had driven my father to seek me out, but his sneering made it harder to feel appreciative. My mother had been worried too, but she had not sneered. Possibly I would get a better chance to explain later.

My prayers were full of hope that night. I could see that Josiah was the great hope of the nation. If anyone could turn the nation to God, he could. Doubts were still there, but on balance, I thought he could do it. Tomorrow, I would try harder to get across the message of imminent destruction. If the people listened and repented, it wouldn't need to happen. Nineveh was living proof of this.

❧

The next day was exhausting. I tried harder. Speaking with all the passion I could muster, I tried to convince my varied audiences of imminent destruction. I failed. There were occasional flickers of response, glimmers of understanding, but only in a few. There was no wholesale acknowledgement of a terrifying vision of horror, and certainly no popular admission of guilt. It was as if God's words were just the latest "interesting idea" to tickle their ears.

As the day progressed, I tried different strategies. I jumped down from my raised platform and walked among the crowd. I spoke God's words directly to individuals and challenged them to respond – and they seemed to think it was part of the show. Live theatre. A new form of entertainment. But I'm not sure that many even noticed the words. On this day, cool and clear, there was no competition from the gusty wind of yesterday, but my words might as well have been blown away for all the effect they had.

Hanamel my cousin was in the crowd on one occasion. Afterwards he congratulated me on my "performance".

Even Azariah deigned to come and listen. He came with some of his friends and stood with them at the edge of the crowd. They didn't throw anything at me, so I suppose I should have been glad about that, but God's word made absolutely no impression on them. That night, Azariah told me that he still couldn't believe that God would speak to a young kid like me.

I tried even harder. I spoke more loudly – until my voice began to fail. I waved my arms and stamped my feet until they hurt. I kept to God's script, but tried to spice it up with emotion and zeal. No-one seemed to listen. The crowds seemed to be entertained rather than confronted. God's threats simply bounced off the hard hearts of his people, rather than finding any way in. Nineveh had repented, but my people would not.

To say that I was disappointed would be like saying that Goliath was quite tall, or that the flood was a minor inconvenience. I was shattered and dejected. What next? Were the people completely stupid? This has been the history of all of my work as a prophet, and the work of most other prophets too. Jonah was an outstanding exception, and there was to be another one who would also be an exception a few years after this time.

During the afternoon, as the sun was declining in the west, I was just delivering the last of God's words to a mostly apathetic crowd at the gate of the temple, when a well-dressed couple approached along the way from the lower part of the city. They listened as I concluded God's words and added the closing words I had started to use to make it clear that these were the words of God, not my own: "So says Yahweh of hosts, the God of Israel." The man walked on through the gates into the temple, but the woman approached me. She looked a little older than my mother, with greying hair and a clear, honest look in her eyes. She smiled as she greeted me, "Peace, young man, did Yahweh really speak to you?"

"Yes, he spoke to me just two days ago and told me to speak these words to the people of Jerusalem," I answered.

"How did he speak to you? Was there a dream, a voice, a messenger? How did it happen? What time of day?" Her eyes were alight with interest.

Before I knew it, I was explaining all of what had happened: the voice, the clouds, the glowing writing in my mind. It was a joy to speak to someone who was interested! Through all of it, she listened with rapt attention, and the smile on her lips slowly grew. It was obvious that she was very pleased to hear my story, and whenever I showed signs of slowing down, she would interpose another question that would start me off again. It was like talking to my mother, but with a feeling of an even greater understanding of the work of God.

My curiosity was growing, and finally I asked, "Why are you so interested in all of this? Who are you?"

"My name is Huldah," she replied, as if that should explain everything. It didn't.

"Why do you ask me about God's messages?" I persisted.

"I too have heard the voice of God," she said. "I too have felt the fire in my bones and known the majesty of his presence. I cannot explain exactly what it is like – you seem to do a better job than I can, young man." She smiled again, and it felt as if we could come closer to God together by talking about him. Sharing that closeness with another human being seemed to make it deeper, somehow. My mother had always been the one who was my closest connection to God; she was most able to share the fear and love for God which I felt in my heart. She had helped to plant it there, and fostered its growth. And now here was someone who seemed even closer to God, and not just because she had heard his voice.

As we continued to share our experiences, hers over years, mine over such a short and painfully recent time, our conversation helped us each to draw nearer to the God we worshipped. Different ages and different life experiences, but a shared target of fellowship with God. Just a few minutes of talking to her helped me to understand more how I felt about God than I had ever done before. Her immovable attachment to Yahweh came through so clearly, and her reasons were so simply expressed. Yahweh was real. Yahweh was present. Yahweh was a loving and generous God who would forgive thousands. But Yahweh was also a jealous and terrifying God who would not clear the guilty. All of this came from her lips as a warm and reassuring manifestation of comfort. It was a complete surprise to me, and just what I needed at that moment. I was not alone.

We talked for quite some time. It seemed so easy to share the conviction that each of us felt, the conviction that there is indescribable beauty in the worship of our God.

Time must have flown by, because it felt like only a minute or two had passed when suddenly the man with whom she had been walking came out of the temple and approached us. She introduced him, saying, "This is Shallum, my husband. He manages the temple wardrobe for the king."

"My wife has been wanting to speak to the new prophet we had heard about," he said, smiling a warm, welcoming smile, just as his wife had. "A new prophet, very new. Are you genuinely a prophet of Yahweh, Jeremiah?"

He knew my name. I wondered how.

"Yahweh has given me a message to speak to his people, so I am doing my best with his help," I replied, "but I don't seem to be communicating it very successfully."

With a broadening smile he responded, "You can't expect to communicate well with a stone, can you?" Then his smile disappeared and he spoke earnestly, "The one you need to speak to is Josiah the King, but they won't let you do that. Huldah is a prophetess and Yahweh has spoken to her too, but she is never allowed to see the King. His minders make sure of that."

"His minders?" I repeated.

"Maaseiah, Shaphan and the rest. None of them want Josiah to hear all the truth from God. They want to filter it so that our young King does nothing 'rash'."

"Oh," was all I could think of to say.

"Well, we must go. Don't give up, young man, but don't be surprised if you can't convince the stony hearts; and don't be surprised if they don't let you get to the one who would actually listen"; he inclined his head towards the palace and rolled his eyes meaningfully.

As they walked away, I wondered how I could find out more about Huldah. Fortunately, she was so much older than me that there would be no trouble caused by asking my father or mother some questions about her. I needed to know who she was and what she did. My few minutes of discussion with her had greatly encouraged me, and her husband's pointed comments had opened my eyes a little more. Josiah was king, but even at 21, he was still being "shepherded". I wondered whether the message God was delivering through me had been presented to the king; and if it had, how much had it been "sanitised" first?

That afternoon I walked home quickly. The rays of the late afternoon sun were turning the tops of the hills a glorious orange-red and the gusty winds of early spring were returning. There was still no rain – which would mean little food for the nation. A farmer is always dependent on the mercy of God, and should be the first to understand the message of withheld rain. Even as priests, my family knew the effects of drought on offerings and the size of gifts made to God. But my discussion with Huldah had highlighted a difference in focus and foundation. Many spoke to me about Yahweh, but none had seemed to view him as their shepherd. Our great king David had written the delightfully evocative words, "Yahweh is my shepherd"[102] yet all who I talked to conveyed the belief that they were in control of their own lives and pleased to have it so. Many had the trappings of religion, but it seemed hollow. God's name was on their lips, but seemed far from their hearts.

As I have grown older I have seen a subtle irony in David's words: sheep only want a shepherd when they feel a need for him. They are glad of their shepherd when they need food or help, but at other times they ignore him and do whatever they want. They actively object when the shepherd directs or regulates their activities, and are very slow to learn what he teaches.

How right Isaiah was when he said, "We all like sheep have gone astray. Each of us has turned to his own way."[103]

Trying harder to bring the people back just didn't seem to be working, but I mustn't give up.

---

[102] Psalm 23:1
[103] Isaiah 53:6

During the evening meal that night, I asked about Huldah the prophetess. My father stopped chewing his mouthful of stew for a moment and looked at me seriously. "Why do you ask about her?" he said, then finished his mouthful. "She is not exactly in favour at the palace. She's a bit of an idealist, even an extremist, I suppose. Her ideas are a little… er… simplistic. Her suggestions don't take into account the realities of modern society."

"I met her at the gate of the temple today," I said, "and we shared our experiences of the presence of God. She has heard words from God over several years. In what way is she an extremist?"

"Well," my father started slowly, appearing to choose his words carefully, "Josiah's nobles have heard from her on many occasions, and I believe they have decided that it is necessary to keep her away from the king."

"Why?" I asked.

My father stroked his beard and thought a while. "God's word is not always simple to understand," he ventured; "amateurs can read it and latch on to the meaning that seems obvious on the face of it, while missing the true underlying wisdom. A literal interpretation of some issues misses the mystical beauty of our God's delicate imagery. At times, for example, God has described his people in ways that appear very critical, even derogatory, and some have taken these to mean that we need to completely reform our society. Yet even the magnificent King David did not set about a complete re-imagining of Israel when he became king. Instead he moved in a slow and steady way. A king who sets a good example leads the nation methodically towards goodness. The sudden changes promoted by extremists can cause confusion, or even open rebellion."

"So why does God express himself so clearly and categorically if he does not want us to take his words at face value?" I asked.

"Ah, my son, my son. This is why God uses the wise heads on the shoulders of elders to rule his nation." A somewhat condescending smile lifted the corners of his mouth, and my father's voice had softened. Now its message touched my ears with all the sweetness of honey to the palate, as he dispensed the priceless wisdom of our fathers. "Age and experience give a kingdom the guidance that avoids an over-hasty realignment of national goals."

It was hard to know how to respond to this while showing proper respect. The nub of the argument seemed to be that old men could stop a nation from changing quickly and that this was, almost by definition, a good thing! It seemed that Jonah was coming to my thoughts quite often these days. He was probably the best practical example of the fallacy of the argument. But somehow, I thought I could guess what the response would be.

"Father, did not the Assyrians change quickly when Jonah warned them? They only had forty days left and changed immediately," I countered, and waited.

The answer came as I had half expected. With a gentle tugging of his beard and the air of giving an obvious answer that still must be explained to a simple child, he said, "Indeed, my son, but they were Gentiles; foreigners who did not have the benefits we have."

As I listened to these words, I felt the fire of God burning within me again. Would he speak to me again or was this just the upwelling of words he had already placed in me?

My father continued, his voice liquid and mellifluous, yet majestic and imposing, "We are descendants of Abraham, benefitting from many generations of the worship of Yahweh. We have Yahweh's temple. We have his words. We are his priests. We do not change our god every year."

His voice reached a crescendo, and as it did so, the fire of God burned white-hot within me, bursting out of my lips in words that could not be contained or softened in their condemnation:

> " 'Has a nation changed its gods,
> even though they are no gods?
> But my people have changed their glory
> for that which does not profit.

> Be appalled, O heavens, at this;
> be shocked, be utterly desolate,
> declares the Lord,
> for my people have committed two evils:
> they have forsaken me,
> the fountain of living waters,
> and hewed out cisterns for themselves,
> broken cisterns that can hold no water.'[104] "

I took a deep breath and tried to calm down as the fire receded a little. "Those are the words of Yahweh our God, my father. Those are the very words he gave me to speak, and has now forced me to say again."

My father was looking shocked. I had never spoken to him like this before, and it had clearly made a deep impression. My mother – oh, my poor mother – was also shocked and bewildered. The question was written clearly on her face: How could things have come to such a pass in her peaceful home?

Azariah and Gemariah looked on in wondering silence and the servants had all gathered to watch.

What could I say? I tried to think of words to smooth things over, but as I did, the fire inside me burned hotter. Silence might be the best option.

"Well, really!" said my father. "Young people nowadays just won't listen to wisdom. Really, Jeremiah, I am very concerned about your attitude. If God was really speaking to you, he would surely teach you respect for your father."

He took another mouthful and the critical moment had passed. The servants went about their business again. Once again, Yahweh had protected me when I held on to his words – although in this case, he had given me no choice about speaking his words! The fire within was burning lower, although some of God's later words to me were running insistently through my head:

> "…you say, 'I am innocent;
> surely his anger has turned from me.'

---

[104] The words of God in Jeremiah 2:11-13.

> Behold, I will bring you to judgment
> for saying, 'I have not sinned.' "[105]

My father wanted to change the subject. "You were asking about Huldah," he said. "I suppose she is a prophetess, but her words are a little inflammatory at times."

I couldn't help smiling to myself at the unintended pun here. God's words were certainly a fire in me – inflammatory was right.

He continued, "Her parents were victims of Manasseh's purges. They were resolute worshippers of God, and one day they simply disappeared. No-one ever knew what happened to them. When Manasseh repented, Huldah was there to give him messages from God, but then he died and Amon became king. It's a risky business being a prophet when times change." He looked at me meaningfully, trying to get across the same message as he had earlier expressed in more oratorical terms.

"Thank you for telling me about her," I replied. "Her experiences haven't dampened her enthusiasm for Yahweh."

"No," my father answered, "and I hope she won't regret it."

We ate in silence for a while. The meal was drawing to an end when I thought again about the scrolls. Several times in the last few days I had promised myself some time reading the scriptures, but the opportunity was elusive. Now the logs in the fire were glowing red and the flames were dancing above the hearth. It would be some time yet before the fire was banked and the family went to their beds. First the servants would eat, and then their work of tidying and cleaning would keep them busy for an hour or so.

"Father," I asked, "what scrolls do we have in the house?" As a family of priests, we had much better access to scrolls of the scriptures than anyone else would, and we normally had several scrolls in the house for various reasons.

"We have Isaiah's prophecy and some of the Psalms," he replied, "but remember what I said. You are young, and young

---

[105] Jeremiah 2:35

people are not well versed in the symbology of the word. You could be led astray and misunderstand or exaggerate…." He seemed about to continue his earlier speech, but apparently thought better of it. I was relieved.

We stood up together and he led me to the special room in which we kept the rolls of God's word. The scrolls were each lovingly wrapped in linen and tied with a leather thong.

"Now, my boy," my father said, "this is a scroll of Isaiah. Of course, it is not the original, but a copy of his words. Many copies were made by the men of King Hezekiah, but most were destroyed by his son. We are quite safe having this scroll now, but if you had been caught with this scroll in the time of Manasseh, it would have cost you your head, and probably the heads of your wife and children too. And your inheritance. Anyway, this scroll was kept safely through the early reign of Manasseh by some very brave men. Of course, it wasn't anyone in our family – it would be a bit too obvious if the High Priest hid such religious scrolls. Our relatives had quite a good working relationship with Manasseh. Through their diplomacy and negotiating skills they kept the temple intact. That alone was worth all the sacrifices required."

"What sacrifices did they make?" I asked.

"Well… I was a little young to understand all that was going on," my father replied lamely, "but many faithful servants of the temple had to sacrifice their positions in society and leave Jerusalem completely for many years. Some sacrificed their wealth to bribe Manasseh's officials to protect innocent people, and others sacrificed their jobs by refusing to fully implement the malicious rules of the king. Of course, the position of High Priest is rather important, and your grandfather had to maintain it as a figurehead, a representative of our national service to Yahweh."

"Did our family ever try to protect the innocent people Manasseh was persecuting? Did we ever try to change Manasseh's direction in life?" I thought I knew the answer, but I had to ask.

The answer was immediate: "Our position in worship and society requires us to represent all the people. We can't focus too much on a small fraction of the people, even when their need is great. The whole nation needs us to represent them before Yahweh – even evil kings like Manasseh. If we had been a family of ordinary priests, rather than the High Priest's family, we could have done such things, but unfortunately our position forbade that. Sometimes the position one must maintain is very constraining."

Immediate, but not convincing.

Obviously my family had collaborated with Manasseh's regime and his reign of terror. Not, perhaps, the full cooperation of complete agreement, but at least the "I'm too scared to stand up against this" sort of cooperation. Knowing that my family was too afraid to make a stand or help others was bad enough, but was it more than that? If Manasseh had taken the possessions and inheritances of so many brave and godly people, why were we so rich?

Suspicions only so far, but I was beginning to ask questions.

Chapter 12

Of Scrolls and Study

Scrolls have a lovely smell – mostly.

Owners take extreme care of scrolls because they are worth so much money. The great value is not because of the material used for the scroll – it is the many hours required to produce an accurate copy. A scroll of Isaiah, such as the one I was now unwrapping, represented up to three months of painstaking, fastidious and methodical work by a skilled scribe. Scrolls were normally kept specially wrapped in linen, and often stored in clay jars in dry rooms, but this was too dangerous in the time of Manasseh. Instead, caves, cisterns and holes in the ground were all used to hide the precious rolls from the watchful eyes of Manasseh's vicious policemen. However, because of the unusual places where scrolls had to be hidden, they sometimes got wet and decay set in. Some were rescued soon enough to avoid any damage to the text, but the corruption left its mark: a stale, musty smell always remained.

This scroll of Isaiah smelled bad. It was a copy made from the original scroll of Isaiah's prophecies just before the end of King Hezekiah's reign, and had been kept through the worst of

Manasseh's ravages by one of the brave men my father had referred to – a priest who had kept it in a clay pot in a cistern which only rarely filled. When heavy rain came, he would take the jar and store it inside his house for a while – taking the risk for as long as necessary. But once, a few years before the Assyrian invasion took Manasseh away, he couldn't rescue the scroll because he was in prison himself. Manasseh had had him arrested on suspicion of heresy – which normally meant that someone was reported to be actively following Yahweh. Talk was cheap and fairly harmless – Manasseh would allow people to talk about Yahweh; but active, visible worship? Never!

After some time spent in a prison cell, the priest was allowed to go free because of a lack of evidence. Very fortunate – protected by God you might say. None of his fellow suspects could be intimidated into acknowledging that he was an active, though cautious, servant of Yahweh. They kept silent throughout the interrogations, accepting the beatings and degradation, until they were all freed, after strident warnings.

Two days before he was granted his freedom, however, he watched in horror as rain tumbled down and the streets ran with sheets of water. He agonised over the danger to the scroll he had risked his life for. What damage could be inflicted on this unspeakably valuable fragment of God's word? He imagined the water cascading over the jar; the ink spreading, dissolving, staining the surface of the scroll. When given his freedom, his first act was to retrieve the pot and examine the damage. In fact, there was surprisingly little damage – good reason to give thanks to God. Nevertheless, the linen had become damp, and two days of sitting in the dampness had caused mould and fungus to begin growing at the edges of the scroll.

As I heard the story told, as soon as this priest arrived home, he risked his life even further by spreading out this scroll across the benches of his house in full view of any who cared to see – a ticket to the grave if the wrong eyes should see it. It was a blessing indeed that no officer of Manasseh chanced that way over the next few days.

Unfortunately, though, while the contents were not affected, the scroll had been damaged in a way that could not be repaired. Decay and mould can cause very unpleasant smells, and this scroll smelled bad.

In ordinary times in the history of Judah, such a scroll would be quickly disposed of, but these were not ordinary times. Few old or original scrolls had survived Manasseh's onslaughts, and the ones which had, had only done so through obscurity. A hidden scroll was a safe scroll. If you wanted to save a scroll, it was safer to hide it somewhere away from your house, so that if someone found it unexpectedly, you would not be suspected. Many scrolls had been hidden in this way, and new discoveries of such treasures were still being made, even thirteen years into Josiah's reign. Slowly, these scrolls were being copied to new scrolls, and once there were enough spare copies, ones like this would be disposed of. But a scribe's work was slow, and besides, who would cover the cost? Copying of contracts and bills of sale paid much better than time spent copying a scroll of Isaiah. Who would pay for it? Some scribes cared enough to use their spare time for such tasks, but most were too busy and the motivation was missing.

So I read the smelly scroll. At first the musty smell was unpleasant in my nostrils, but it didn't take long to get used to it, and it was worth it. The room was dim, with just a single lamp keeping the darkness at bay. I sat on a small stool with the scroll spread out on the bench before me, the lamp resting in a small nook in the wall so that its light would fall on the unrolled part of the scroll.

I wasn't looking for anything in particular, just reading to learn. God's words against the priests had left me feeling that I must do something myself to learn more of his words – not just the words he had spoken directly to me, but the words he had written for all.

Isaiah had spoken words from God through the time of four kings of Judah, some good and some bad. Many of his prophecies I had read before during my schooling, and found very hard to understand. Still, understanding wasn't going to come if I didn't read it, so it was time to start.

Reading the start of Isaiah was just like hearing God's words to me all over again. The message was just the same. Evil and rebellion. Sin and ignorance. Even the context was much the same. Uzziah was a good king – except for an attack of pride when he tried to usurp the job of the priests. God had punished him for that presumption with life-long leprosy. Overall, however, we judged him to be a good king: Godly, righteous and true. Yet the words of Yahweh through Isaiah condemned:

> "Ah, sinful nation, a people laden with iniquity,
> offspring of evildoers, children who deal corruptly!
> They have forsaken the Lord,
> they have despised the Holy One of Israel,
> they are utterly estranged."[106]

Why, why, why? Surely a good king was a reason for God to be pleased? I read and re-read the first section several times, striving for understanding. As my fingers played with the discoloured edges of the scroll, the mildewy smell wafted through the room, but I barely noticed. Why would God condemn the nation so strongly when a good king was doing the best he could? Was my father right? Was God just exaggerating to get our attention – using hyperbole to make people sit up and take notice? Was I just too young and simple to understand? The light of my lamp flickered as a gust of wind made the shutters rattle and the shadows dance dimly on the wall. And then it struck me: some words Isaiah had spoken about God's attitudes or thoughts. What were they? It seemed that they must be important, and my mind struggled to capture the memory. Thoughts... actions. God's thoughts... God's actions. I almost had the words; I pushed my mind to reach out, to struggle and grasp them... but they eluded me as thoughts are wont to do. I gave up and bent over the scroll again, skipping the initial criticism of Israel. My eyes fell on the next column as my fingers felt the smooth, dry, coolness of the leather, scraped and re-scraped as it had been during manufacture to make sure it was completely smooth and easy to write on. The text read:

---

[106] Isaiah 1:4

"…many peoples shall come, and say:
'Come, let us go up to the mountain of the Lord,
to the house of the God of Jacob,
that he may teach us his ways
and that we may walk in his paths.'
For out of Zion shall go the law,
and the word of the Lord from Jerusalem."[107]

I knew that Isaiah was full of prophecies of better times, future times when the whole world would acknowledge Yahweh as the creator. These would be times when all nations would come to Jerusalem and Abraham would really be the "father of many nations". Well, they obviously hadn't happened in the lifetime of Isaiah, nor at any time since. The only reason other nations came near Judah now was to harass us or to attempt to drum up local support for a united opposition to any of the greater powers: Egypt, Assyria or Babylon. No-one came to visit the temple. No-one came to learn the ways of God – and then I had it: the idea that had been eluding me.

God's ways. There was something comparing or contrasting God's ways with our human ways. Where was it? One thing I was sure of was that it was towards the end of the roll. I remembered reading it during a lesson with Immer, my teacher, about a year ago – or maybe two. I still remembered his less than complimentary reflections on the way I had been rolling and re-rolling the scroll. "Not like that, Jeremiah, not like that! You look as if you are trying to tear it in half!" he had said. "Give slowly and take gently. Like this"; and he showed me the way to slowly unroll the next part of the scroll with my left hand and gently take up the extra on the earlier part of the scroll with my right hand. There is a skill in handling scrolls and a careless reader can take years off the life of a scroll. A smooth shape in the two rolls, smooth and not too tight; this makes a happy scribe. Taking Immer's advice to heart, I had learned to handle a scroll to his satisfaction. Of course, that was why I was now allowed to read a valuable scroll like this by myself. So now, with proper care, I unrolled and re-rolled the scroll until I was near the end.

---

[107] Isaiah 2:3

All scrolls have character. A scribe can choose to follow the conventional methods of writing, with columns of a fixed width, lines of a fixed height and letters of a fixed size and generic style; or his foibles can show through. Little extra decorations or special marks to draw attention to texts the scribe thought especially important – these variations can make the difference between a scroll feeling like an intimate friend, or merely a cold acquaintance. Some scribes did the work as skilled and well-paid professionals, producing beautiful but bland results. For them, it was simply a job: get it done, and get paid. To other scribes, however, the opportunity to write the words of God was a labour of love and an almost overwhelming responsibility. The weeks or months of work bound up in a scroll make each one an adventure in the exploration of motivation. A scroll is an opportunity to showcase the work of an artist, to produce a magnum opus, a treasure that would be cherished for generations after its crafter was dead. What a tragedy that this scroll, so beautiful in presentation and intimate in decoration, the loving work of a master craftsman, should be left unwanted because of water damage.

As I came nearer to the end of the scroll I skimmed the text, trying to find the words I was looking for. God's ways. Our ways. It took quite some time, but eventually I found it:

> "For my thoughts are not your thoughts,
> neither are your ways my ways, declares the Lord.
> For as the heavens are higher than the earth,
> so are my ways higher than your ways
> and my thoughts than your thoughts."[108]

Was this the hint I was looking for? God's ways being so much higher than our ways? If we think someone is good, God must still think they have a long way to go. Could it be that God was actually showing his approval of Josiah by raising his requirements? When teaching me how to handle scrolls, Immer had started very gently. His expectations were low at first; but once I started to learn, he raised his expectations, and carelessness that he would initially have tolerated as ignorance,

---

[108] Isaiah 55:8-9

later became the target of pointed criticism. Maybe this was God's method too.

Judah had been blessed with a "good" king in Uzziah when Isaiah was prophesying, and God's words against the behaviour of the nation sounded quite harsh. Now Judah had another "good" king, and the message I was to deliver was very similar to what Isaiah had said. A better king seemed to mean higher expectations. Josiah and the whole nation were being dragged up towards godliness, and the steps that had been taken served chiefly to highlight how much more work still had to be done. Not only that, but God was trying to give the warning to someone who would take notice. Destruction would inevitably come if Judah did not serve God. Manasseh (for most of his reign) and Amon would never have believed this – although God still sent them warnings by many prophets. But now there was a king whose ears were open, and God was making it clear just how bad the situation was. Indeed, how far down the path Judah had already travelled, sometimes walking, sometimes running, but almost always heading downwards to destruction.

I had straightened up as I thought this through and was staring unseeing at the guttering lamp. The wind had been rising as the thoughts had been tumbling around in my head, and now the feeble flame was flickering so much that it was struggling to keep alight. As I write now, the reasoning seems very clear and simple, but it was a great struggle when I first started to understand more about God's expectations. Because he is so far above us in his ways, yet so loving and patient, he tailors his demands to our current situation. As Isaiah said of God, "we are the clay, and you are our potter; we are all the work of your hand."[109] A potter shapes each pot individually, his fingers pressing, moulding, applying just the force needed for each pot, depending on how the clay was initially shaped. As the shape of the pot gets closer to what the potter requires, the demands seem greater, but the changes needed are smaller. A lump of clay newly thrown onto the wheel is not expected to have a smooth and even finish, but as the process of shaping

---

[109] Isaiah 64:8

and working proceeds, the expectations grow as the shape of the pot approaches the final goal.

God's warnings about coming destruction were real. Manasseh's behaviour had guaranteed that. Maybe Josiah was being warned in this way because it was in his power to change the nation. God's threats were made to him because he was righteous enough to listen and want to make changes.

Would he listen? Would his minders even let him hear?

Finally, the wind achieved what it had long threatened – the lamp flickered out. Sitting in the darkness, I realised that if I could not convince Josiah, my nation would surely be snuffed out just like the lamp. I must do my best to make him hear.

That night in my prayers I continued to ask God, and to wonder. Was there any hope, or would my nation soon be destroyed? At that time, I had no idea that it would be forty long years before the destruction came. Nor did I know that destruction was indeed inevitable, simply because no-one would listen.

CR

Scrolls took up my evenings from that night on. Daytime found me in Jerusalem, looking for an audience, trying to find someone who would really listen. Evenings took me through the scrolls of the prophets, the Psalms, and the history of Abraham, Isaac and Jacob. Scrolls from the library in the temple were always available to trainee priests like me, and there never seemed to be much demand anyway. I suppose the lack of demand proved God's words:

> "The priests did not say, 'Where is the Lord?'
> Those who handle the law did not know me."[110]

New scrolls were also available for use in the temple, but I couldn't bring these home with me due to the possibility of rain, and I genuinely preferred the older scrolls anyway. A scroll is only as good as the scribe who wrote it, and I had more

---

[110] Jeremiah 2:8

confidence in scribes who were long dead, those from the time of King Hezekiah or even earlier. Once I started to make enquiries about such scrolls, I began to find that there were quite a few available, and no one else seemed to want them anyway. Students wanted nice new scrolls, and there was also an understanding that the old scrolls conveyed messages that were more demanding than those in the new scrolls.

During the day, I also spent some time in the temple area. Comparing new scrolls with old scrolls took a lot of time, but was very rewarding. Over time, I found that the old scrolls portrayed God as a loving but jealous God. The new scrolls, however, mostly portrayed him as a loving and tolerant God. The passages of judgement had lost their fire. God's threats of punishment for sin had been watered down. This discovery sparked a determination in me to do what I could to bring back the old ways, the messages of the old scrolls which had a ring of truth – and fitted with God's words as I had experienced them.

One day, while reading a new and particularly beautiful scroll that seemed to suggest God was perfectly happy for his people to worship other gods, it occurred to me to wonder whether the purification of our libraries would be part of God's work for me. It would be a very challenging job, and could only be done if I became completely familiar with all the messages God had given to his people. A massive undertaking, but one I felt I should work towards. If God gave messages to his people, they must be worth knowing – and more than that, they must be worth understanding.

Immer, my teacher, had asked me to come and discuss my new direction in life. How many people would there be who would try to discourage me from doing God's work? Immer's words told me that being God's prophet was good, but the meaning he conveyed was quite different. Prophets, he implied, were immature, ignorant, dangerous and arrogant. Immature, because they were childishly simplistic in their attitudes; ignorant, because they did not recognise that God simply does not rule the nations, but has left it up to men; dangerous, because they tried to inspire a religious fervour that stirred up discrimination and hatred; arrogant, because they believed they were the only ones with a direct line of communication to God, and were therefore holier than everyone else. I had never been on the receiving end of such a lecture in my life. I could not identify criticism in any specific words, but the meaning was as obvious as the full moon on a clear night. It was masterful, and made me question again what I was doing. This was happening so often it was becoming discouraging. No-one agreed with me. No-one supported me.

It would have been easy to lapse into the depths of self-pity in those days, but when I felt tempted to do so, I would remember that it was not quite true to say that no-one supported me. My mother had offered some cautious support, but it was limited by her loyalty to her husband. Huldah's was the only unqualified support and she continued to seek me out every few days. I found talking to her about Yahweh inspiring, because he was so real to her – unlike all those who were trying to discourage me. She worshipped a living God. The others seemed to worship a god who could be shaped and constrained, limited and controlled. Lip-service only. Our scriptures tell us that Yahweh created us in his image, but most people who said they worshipped him seemed to want to create him in their image. Did they fear him or his threats of punishment? I don't believe they ever did. Even when his words came true, I don't think they believed it was his work.

Immer and Huldah are both long dead now. They died at much the same time, during the first attack of Nebuchadnezzar the Chaldean: but one died in terror, while the other died in peace because she knew that her God was in control. When there is terror on every side, peace can only come from within.

℘

Since I had spent the majority of each day in Jerusalem speaking to crowds, many thousands of people must now have heard the message Yahweh had given me. But nothing seemed to have changed. Audiences all over the city had heard the words, and even those in areas outside the walls where many of the poorer people lived. The poor would be the first to suffer when the attack came from the north.

These were also the areas in which the worship of many false gods was most popular. Hills were favoured as places for pagan altars – even Solomon himself had built high places to satisfy his wives' cravings for the gods they had known as children. The Mount of Corruption was a good name for that whole area, and none of Josiah's reforms had touched it yet.

Shrines which nestled beneath leafy green trees were no less in demand. Even valleys like the Valley of the Son of Hinnom, where ready supplies of water helped to wash away the blood of slaughtered innocents, and ample fuel burned their pathetic corpses to ash; such places were appallingly fashionable.

It was in that valley, in Topheth, that I had my first experience of violence in response to God's word. Of all the accursed places of pagan worship, Topheth was the worst. No-one knows how many children have met their dooms on its altars while drums covered up the screams.

Many potters work near a gate of Jerusalem which leads to Topheth, so much so that the gate is called the Potsherd Gate[111]. It seems like it should be a simple thing to make pots, but huge numbers end up broken after firing, and they don't have much use except as cheap "paper" for teaching children to write. As I walked past the potters at their work that day, I felt a little envious of them with their clearly defined profession, producing pots every day for eager customers, whilst I walked the path of uncertainty as an unpopular prophet. In the days immediately before, a struggle had been playing out in my mind. "Speak to Jerusalem". Did that include Topheth? After all, the Valley of the Son of Hinnom was outside the walls, and thus, technically, outside Jerusalem. Sometimes I could just dismiss it from my mind, but the thought would always come back, gnawing at the edge of my consciousness until it had gained my full attention. Should I, or shouldn't I? Worshippers of Baal and the other gods of the nations around, murderers of their own children though they were, even these should hear the word of Yahweh. I knew that it was fear that fuelled the argument which sought to give me a clear

---

[111] Jeremiah 19:2

conscience while still avoiding Topheth. But the warning words of God still nagged at me:

> "Do not be dismayed by them,
> lest I dismay you before them."[112]

After a few days of this mental harrying, I gave in and went to Topheth, but I didn't feel much like a "fortified city, an iron pillar, and bronze walls" as I walked past the piles of potsherds and down into the valley. In some ways it was almost like entering another world. Down there, there was not even a pretence of serving Yahweh. Altars, shrines and carved images were everywhere.

It happened in the middle of Yahweh's words, and I suppose it was predictable where it would happen:

> "How can you say, 'I am not unclean,
> I have not gone after the Baals'?
> Look at your way in the valley;
> know what you have done—
> a restless young camel running here and there,
> a wild donkey used to the wilderness,
> in her heat sniffing the wind!
> Who can restrain her lust?"[113]

The audience had been a bit raucous right from the start. Some of them had obviously heard my words before and were stirring up trouble before I got very far. But when it came to references to Baal and the valley, to the comparison of idolaters with young camels in heat, that's when they snapped.

Shouts broke out and the air was full of abuse. Words I had never even heard before were screamed at me, and several men began bending to pick up stones. It was lucky for me that there were no larger stones to be had, or I probably wouldn't have got out alive. No big stones, perhaps, but gravel was there in abundance and a lot of it began to fly in my direction. It wasn't likely to kill, but I can tell you it didn't feel good! I lurched back a little, but it didn't occur to me to turn and run.

---

[112] Jeremiah 1:17

[113] Jeremiah 2:23-24

In fact, I even kept shouting the message from God. In all likelihood, it would have gone very badly for me if a pagan procession hadn't chosen just that time to walk up the valley, sounding their cymbals, bells and drums. The so-called priests told the troublemakers to stop the melee, and the dust soon began to settle. I was saved – with just a few bruises to remind me of the nearness of my escape.

Chapter 13

King Josiah

King Josiah raised his arm. Half a dozen men stepped forward, surrounding the altar. At one corner, near the stairs, their leader took his position. After flexing his fingers a few times on the shaft of his sledgehammer, he lifted it off his shoulder and swung. Slowly the heavy sledge rose, seemed almost to pause for an instant, then plunged with terrible speed towards the target. Metal struck stone with a dull, solid thud. He had chosen his target well: a small spurt of dust arose, shards of shattered stone peppered the watching crowd, and a large crack opened in the rock. Teetering on the edge of the stone beneath, the fractured wedge swayed backward and forward once or twice before sliding off and falling to the pavement.

A gasp rose from the crowd, while muted cheers came from a few. My involuntary cheer earned me some unpleasant looks, particularly from the white-robed priests who had served at this doomed altar to Baal.

Another of Josiah's demolition team raised his sledgehammer, and suddenly all of them were showering heavy blows on the damaged altar. Clouds of dust were rising and flying fragments made it hazardous to stay too close. Other workers were also standing by, holding thick branches, and from time to time the sledgehammer crew would step back and the branches would be pushed into the newly-opened gaps between stones and used to lever the battered stones apart until they fell off the shrinking altar. A jumble of stones soon littered the walkway and the crowd was starting to warm up. Violent destruction always pleases a crowd, and after a time, applause rose with each displaced stone.

My emotions were mixed. Joy came with the obliteration of this site of pagan worship; but a sceptical, almost cynical disappointment followed the response of the mob. Destruction was easy to cheer, but would the crowd have been just as happy if someone had been knocking down God's altar or God's house? Cheers for dismantling Baal worship today, but what about tomorrow? I knew there was an Asherah pole in the next street, exquisitely carved and skilfully painted. How many of these onlookers would be gathered around it later today or tomorrow? Bowing down, chanting her name, murmuring vows to a dead lump of wood?

Josiah stood and watched the events. This was the closest I had ever been to the king and I was able to study him closely. In his youth, King David had been described as handsome, having red cheeks and beautiful eyes. Josiah fitted this description well. Standing straight and tall, he was sumptuously clothed in a purple cloak. His face was serious but didn't look unaccustomed to smiling. Young, but obviously familiar with command, he gave his orders in a clear, definite tone. There was no mistaking what he wanted!

But what did the watchers want?

A very few had come to revel in the destruction of a symbol of idolatry. These were the ones who had cheered when the initial assault was made on the altar.

Others were their direct opponents. These had come in the hope that they could do something to stop the desecration of their altar. On this occasion, they had failed – but they would not give up.

The majority of the onlookers were there merely to revel in destruction. These were the citizens who would gather for executions and punishments, for the seizure of houses and property as perfected by Manasseh, and for house fires or other disasters. They were not on Josiah's side – God's side – at all, except when he gave them spectacles to satisfy their appetite. Any other violent exhibition would have done just as well, while the worship of idols would be more likely to gratify their other cravings than would the pure worship of Yahweh. On the outside, it looked as if they supported this cleansing of the city, but underneath? I was not so sure.

The men with sledgehammers had almost finished their work now. Instead of course upon course of neatly dressed stones, the altar was reduced to disorganised rubble, the stones no longer squared and shaped. Those with long poles were making sure that not one stone was left standing upon another.

Josiah looked on in approval, standing a little apart from four of the six "mysterious men" whom I now knew. Achbor, Shaphan, Maaseiah and Asaiah had found places to sit, a little away from where the action was. As I looked at Asaiah, our eyes met and it was clear that he recognised me. Did he still hate me? There was no way to tell, but obviously he wasn't jumping up to walk over and talk to me!

In the two weeks since we had first met, I had seen Asaiah and the others from time to time near the king's palace, but none of the six had come to listen again to God's word. These men were Josiah's eyes and ears, his closest advisers – and they had said they would tell him of God's message. No request had come for me to visit the palace, yet I was confident that the message would have got a swift response from Josiah if delivered in full. So, what had they told him? It seemed to me that these men must not wish Josiah to hear the whole message. Should they be allowed to get their own way?

I had joined the audience today to try to stop them getting what they wanted. Josiah must hear the words of Yahweh, and this was an opportunity to make sure he did. Others might have come to rejoice at the destruction, or to see if they could stop it, but I had come to deliver God's message again. Josiah, though king, was nevertheless one of the "people of Jerusalem" who was to hear the word of the Lord, so hear it he must.

It seemed that Maaseiah had suspected what I would be thinking, as he seemed to be keeping an eye on me. There was little left of the altar now, and I started to move towards a small wall on which I could stand. Immediately, Maaseiah advanced to intercept me before I could reach the wall. Achbor and Shaphan had obviously been watching me too, for they also moved silently towards me with two or three soldiers by their side. A fortunate opening had become a trap.

I stopped; but the nobles didn't. Changing their course to meet me, they quickly surrounded me, and Maaseiah greeted me quietly, "Jeremiah, don't do anything that will cause a disturbance. This work is very important to King Josiah, and he does not want any unnecessary disruption which may cause civil unrest. Keep quiet!"

What should I do? If my king wanted me to keep quiet, should I not do so? Would my message actually reduce the effectiveness of Josiah's wonderful work if I delivered it now? After all, surely God would want me to deliver his words in the best way possible? But was this request from Josiah, or did it spring from the agile minds of his nobles? I looked across at Josiah – no help there: he was busy giving instructions about the removal of the small incense altar that sat in a niche looking down on the main altar. Racked with dismay and indecision, I looked from Maaseiah to Achbor, and then to Shaphan. They said nothing, and their faces were serious but almost without expression. What would happen if I started to speak now? How far would I get? On the other hand, if I didn't speak now, would I ever get another opportunity to make Josiah hear?

My mind was in turmoil, but the words of God resounded like a warning bell: "I make you this day a fortified city, an iron pillar, and bronze walls...."[114]   Fortified cities could not be pushed around, they were immovable. God wanted me to be like that and would help me if I was. What if I let them intimidate me into silence? God had warned me; "do not be dismayed by them, lest I dismay you before them."[115]

So a young, insignificant seventeen-year-old rejected the demands of the most important nobles in Judah and called out the words of Yahweh:

"Thus says the Lord,
'I remember the devotion of your youth,
your love as a bride,
how you followed me in the wilderness,
in a land not sown.
Israel was holy to the Lord,
the firstfruits of his harvest.'[116] "

Familiar words now, yet within me the fire still burned and each word glowed, its letters shining as if formed with the flames of individual lamps. The wall in my mind still showed clearly every word God had spoken to me, but I was becoming more used to them and they distracted me less. I could notice more clearly the actions of those around me, and the reactions of Josiah's nobles were worth noticing. Maaseiah initially looked furious and lifted his hand as if to strike me, but then let it fall again to his side. Then he turned and looked towards Josiah, just as the king heard the words and turned.

Quick to hear, but slow to speak. Not many people are like that, let alone kings or nobles, but Josiah was. His nobles waited for his response, and I continued to follow God's script until I came to:

" '...As a thief is shamed when caught,
so the house of Israel shall be shamed:
they, their kings, their officials,
their priests, and their prophets,
who say to a tree, "You are my father,"

---

[114] Jeremiah 1:18
[115] Jeremiah 1:17
[116] Jeremiah 2:2-3

and to a stone, "You gave me birth."
For they have turned their back to me,
and not their face.'[117] "

At the mention of "kings", Josiah responded at last.

"Who are you?" he asked. "And what authority do you have to speak like this?"

Maaseiah answered before I could speak, "My lord, King Josiah, this is the prophet we mentioned to you. He comes from a family of priests in Anathoth, and...."

Josiah motioned with his hand to still the interruption, and asked again, "Who are you?"

"I am Jeremiah, my lord," I replied. "I come from Anathoth and I prophesy coming destruction at the command of Yahweh our God. He sent me to say of our people:

" '...they have turned their back to me,
and not their face.
But in the time of their trouble they say,
"Arise and save us!"
But where are your gods
that you made for yourself?
Let them arise, if they can save you,
in your time of trouble;
for as many as your cities
are your gods, O Judah.'[118] "

Right to the very end of God's words, Josiah listened carefully, making no more interruptions. I felt for him as I said the last words:

" 'Have you not just now called to me,
"My father, you are the friend of my youth—
will he be angry forever,
will he be indignant to the end?"
Behold, you have spoken,
but you have done all the evil that you could.'[119] "

---

[117] Jeremiah 2:26-27
[118] Jeremiah 2:27-28
[119] Jeremiah 3:4-5

"Is that fair, Jeremiah?" King Josiah asked. "Have I done all the evil I can?"

"My lord, these are the words of Yahweh," I answered simply.

"Are they?" he rejoined. "I will have to think more about them. Can you come with me to the palace now?"

Maaseiah interrupted again, "But, my lord, the representatives of the incense manufacturers are coming to meet you. Even now, they will be at the palace waiting for you. If your work here is finished, should we not return to meet them?"

Josiah turned back to look at the remains of the altar. Already many of the larger stones had been loaded onto a cart for disposal. When ordering the desecration and destruction of pagan altars, Josiah always made sure that the surrounds were tidied up so that there was no indication that an altar had ever been there, and no way of simply reassembling the scattered stones – they were taken away. Within days, a public facility – often a latrine – would be built on the spot so that the local community would benefit from the demolition. What Josiah had to assess now was whether enough work had been done for him to be assured that the rest would follow. Josiah had already found that if he didn't monitor such situations carefully, the removal work would not be completed and the remains of the altar would become a rallying point for those who opposed his plan of purifying worship in Jerusalem.

Apparently he decided that enough had been done, for he responded to Maaseiah, "Yes, we must return to the palace, but don't you think Jeremiah's message is more important than discussions about incense? However, I said I would meet them, so I must." Maaseiah looked pleased, satisfied that I had been dispensed with, but Josiah turned to me, "Jeremiah, I need to talk to you more about God's words. Come with me to the palace."

The pleased expression slid off Maaseiah's face and the look he directed at me was anything but pleasant. He had hoped to get rid of me without giving me any chance of a personal audience with the king.

After giving brief instructions to the supervisor of the team that was still tidying up the altar area, Josiah led the way to the palace. Deep in conversation with his nobles, he paid no attention to me, and I trailed along behind, thankful to God that I had been able to get King Josiah's attention, but wondering what it would all lead to. Maaseiah had not been at all happy, and making enemies of the king's favourites did not seem like a good idea.

ᚷ

The king's palace in Jerusalem was very close to the temple of Yahweh, so I was familiar with its appearance, but I had never been inside. As we walked down towards the imposing buildings which represented the construction work of the kings of Judah over hundreds of years, the difference was marked. In the temple area, the stonework needed cleaning and some exposed stones were crumbling and needed replacing. Thinking back over what I knew of the kings in the last couple of centuries, few had lavished any care on God's house, and even now there were no teams of masons or craftsmen coming and going through the gates. By contrast, the king's palace had received plenty of love and attention, and it showed.

The gates of the palace were open, but squads of armed guards stood both inside and out. Josiah's vanguard had been marching ahead of us, and were standing on the stairs leading up to the main entrance as we entered the gates. There was a guard at either end of each step, spears pointing to the sky. As we climbed the stairs between the twin walls of soldiers, Josiah and his nobles paid no attention, but I was feeling a little nervous. Spears and swords were not my tools of trade, and these guards were all fit young men who looked as if they were expert with their weapons – and completely ready to use them. This concentration on security had begun with Manasseh's brush with the Assyrians, and almost 20 years later, Josiah continued it. Garrisons were still maintained in all the major cities of Judah, and their walls were kept in good repair. So why was the temple receiving less attention – less love?

Across a wide porch we walked, and through a pair of large doors that shone with the gleam of burnished metal. Once inside, we made our way along corridors lined with rich hangings and lit with many lamps, until we found ourselves in a chamber with a massive throne at the far end. This must be the throne fashioned by the wise King Solomon, made completely of ivory[120]. On either end of each of the six steps, a carved lion stood – a reminder that the kingdom of Israel had originally included twelve tribes, not just the two that now remained as the kingdom of Judah. When Solomon initially made this throne, it had been completely coated with gold, but the gold had been removed from the throne and replaced several times: removed in Judah's times of weakness, to pay off attacking kings; eventually replaced in times of strength and wealth by later kings of Judah. At this stage of Josiah's reign, there was no gold on the steps, and only a little on selected parts of the footstool and chair as decoration. Even without the gold, though, it was a magnificent throne, and enormous quantities of gold would be required to do the job properly.

Josiah climbed the stairs and sat, alone, on his throne. It seems a little too obvious to require mentioning, but a throne is meant to emphasise the primacy of a king, and it worked. Josiah looked to be in command – a young king, but a king with authority. Remembering the comments of Huldah's husband about Josiah's "minders", I wondered, was Josiah really in control? I decided to suspend judgement.

Everyone except me seemed to know their place. I stood alone near the entrance and for a while it seemed as if I had been forgotten, then Josiah suddenly turned towards me and said, "Jeremiah, one of the chairs to the left of the throne would be the best place for you to wait. I need to talk to these people for a few minutes and then I would like to have you explain your message."

I took a seat as directed, and found myself sitting among the very nobles who had wanted to keep me away from Josiah. Fortunately, they were occupied with a discussion of the subject which so absorbed the visitors now being admitted to the

---

[120] 1 Kings 10:18-20; 2 Chronicles 9:17-19

throne room.   The manufacture of incense seemed a completely unimportant issue to me, but that only reflected my ignorance.   Incense is used in worship. Josiah was destroying the altars to Baal and their associated incense altars. Fundamentally, this business was affected by religion.   The income of incense makers was being reduced by Josiah's attempts to reform the religion of his kingdom, and they didn't like it.

Education cannot cover everything – much knowledge and many ideas must be left out. I had learned much about books, laws, writing, sacrifices and all sorts of details relating to my future employment, but economics had never made an appearance in the syllabus. In looking back now, I can see the hand of God in this small incident.   Never before had it occurred to me that purifying the worship of God would have an impact on people's livelihood.

The representatives of the incense makers were quite insistent on this point: Business was suffering. Supplies of the types of incense used in Baal worship were now a glut on the market.   People in Jerusalem were becoming more cautious about being seen to worship Baal, possibly even a little afraid. Prices were dropping, goods were languishing in stockpiles, and growers could not be paid as the sales were not providing the money they once had.   At the same time, there was no matching increase in the sale of incense for the worship of Yahweh. It was all one way – downhill.

As I sat listening to their arguments, my mind started to walk in areas it had never explored before.   My father's references to priests being guides to kings only considered part of the real situation. Priests could offer kings teaching and instruction in the laws of God – that was their job. But the job of a king was to integrate those laws into the fabric of their kingdom so that their subjects could live in holiness and faithfulness, but also in security while living productive lives. It occurred to me that I was watching the words of Solomon being fulfilled: "…it is the glory of kings to search things out."[121]   Josiah was asking careful questions, listening

---

[121] Proverbs 25:2

thoughtfully to the answers – searching out all the details of this matter.

The leader of the incense sellers was a portly man with thin greying hair and a double chin poorly hidden beneath his straggly beard. He was not trying to understand anything – he already knew. In his mind, the matter was simple: his father and grandfather had sold incense for the worship of many gods over many years. He was not involved in the worship of these gods, all he was doing was trying to put food in his family's mouths, and all this nonsense about "good religion" and "bad religion" was making his family poor. His supporters all had similar stories, and their request to the king was: "Please stop!"

Surely many kings would have given them short shrift and sent them away with a stern message. But Josiah was trying to find a solution which could help these men and their families, while still continuing his purge of idolatry: mixing compassion with purity as King David had so often done. Many suggestions were made by Josiah's advisors, and some practical ideas started to emerge. Josiah would not commit in any way to stopping his "interference"; on the contrary, he mentioned several times his commitment to stamping out the worship of Baal and Asherah. With this emphasis came his advice to the delegation that they would need to take their business in different directions from now on. Religion would be changing, so business would be changing as well, and they were being given clear notice of this. Their current stockpiles of mixed incense would have to be written off or exported to other countries. Some of the ingredients, however, were required for worship in the temple, and Josiah made it clear that this demand would increase as the worship of Yahweh became more important again. At one stage, I was asked about the current use of incense by the priests, but I knew nothing of this and could not answer the question. Josiah's advisors took note of these questions and undertook to make further investigations as to what quantities of the available excess ingredients would be required given the changes in national worship which Josiah was intending.

Josiah closed the audience with a stern warning to the delegation, "Never try to separate your business from your worship. Business is life, and life is worship. The special incense you have been providing is only used for the worship of Baal, and you know that. Assisting in the worship of Baal is truly worship of Baal. Don't make a living by supporting evil."

In that audience alone, Josiah had taught me much. His earnest commitment to God came through so clearly that it could not be questioned. After my musings on the subject, this was a great relief. More surprisingly, his approach to his subjects had opened my eyes. Responsibility is important. It was an important part of being a priest – I knew that. Now I had seen that Josiah viewed himself as being responsible for his subjects, his entire nation. A shepherd must care for his sheep, both as a flock and as individuals, and Josiah felt he must do the same for all his people. No wonder God had used the word "shepherd" when talking about rulers – it was what he expected of them.

Not completely happy, but at least a little mollified, the incense purveyor's collective finally went about their business and Josiah turned directly to Maaseiah: "Approach Hilkiah the priest about the components of incense. I know the incense used in the temple uses a special recipe, but if the ingredients can be obtained from an existing stockpile, that will help everyone." Maaseiah acknowledged the king's words and immediately left the throne room.

In that matter at least, Josiah had convinced me that he was in control of the kingdom.

Turning to me, Josiah said, "Now, Jeremiah, tell me more. How did you receive this message from Yahweh?"

Without describing every detail of the experience, I tried to briefly describe the overwhelming presence of God and how his voice had delivered the frightening message. Realistically, I had no proof, so Josiah would have to take the message on trust – or ignore it. Josiah listened carefully, and at the end he turned to Achbor and Shaphan, "Did you know this?" he asked.

Achbor had the grace to look a little uncomfortable as he replied, "Ah, yes, some of it, my lord." Shaphan returned the king's look impassively, but did not seem eager to contribute.

Josiah pursed his lips and then continued, "You gave me a very brief description of the message of Jeremiah and where it came from. What I now hear does not seem to fit very well. You said it was 'just another vague, fluffy message,' or something like that, didn't you? And that he was, 'a trainee priest with confused dreams.' "

Josiah looked thoughtfully at his embarrassed nobles for quite a while as they sat in abashed silence. He was obviously wondering whether this was something more than just a temporary lapse of judgement on their part.

"My lord, we wished to make some more enquiries before bothering you with something that might be unimportant," said Shaphan, but his heart clearly wasn't in it and he didn't sound convincing.

"So what enquiries have you made since then?" asked Josiah.

"Ah, well… none, my lord, I'm afraid," Shaphan replied. "We have been very busy with many other matters," he finished feebly.

"If Jeremiah's message is genuine, it is utterly critical that I hear it. You can see that, can't you?" said Josiah. As an admirer of Josiah, I was always impressed by his ways of speaking, but this was one of the most skilful little speeches I ever heard him make. Somehow, he managed to make this reproof sound both stern and appealing. It felt to me as though the nobles were being told off, but in a way that encouraged them to do better. The words explained their error, but also showed Josiah's continuing trust in them, suggesting that he knew they would do better in the future. He finished his words with a slightly crooked half-smile at the older men, and the subject was closed as he turned back to me.

As Josiah sat on his throne and did his best to impress his will on the older men who had guided him since he was a young boy, I pictured in my mind's eye the eight-year-old boy king, perched on that massive throne. A boy equipped with all supposed authority, but having no knowledge and a great need of guidance. It was very easy to understand why these older men still found it difficult to loosen the apron strings. In all but name, they had ruled the kingdom, and now Josiah was forcing them to relinquish their power to its rightful owner. This struggle would obviously continue for some time.

King Josiah then had me repeat all the words God had spoken to me, and when I finished, he responded, "You said again that I have done all the evil that I can. Did Yahweh really say that? I do want to worship him in purity." He leaned forward with a puzzled look on his face: "We destroyed an altar to Baal today – surely God would be pleased with that?"

Should I ask him about the condition of the temple and about what took place within its walls? No, there would be time enough for that later.

"My lord, the king," I answered, "if you call on God in honesty, then those words will not apply to you. But what about the bystanders? What about your workers? What about the priests of Yahweh – where were they when they should have been celebrating the destruction of evil? Where will the people worship tomorrow? In the temple of Yahweh? Or at another of the altars to Baal which are in every street?"

"Ah, yes," he said, sighing heavily and leaning back in his throne. Then he asked softly, as if speaking to himself: "How can the hearts of the people be led back to Yahweh?"

Chapter 14

Toward the North

June, 626BC – the 13th year of Josiah

Time passed. Josiah's reforms continued – he at least was genuine. But what of the people? Was this a national reformation, or a national deception?

I had been repeating God's message in Jerusalem for three months now, much longer than I had originally planned or expected. Spring had brought warmth and growth to the surrounding hills, and now the heat of summer was beginning. There were no more cold gusty winds, and I no longer needed to wrap my cloak quite so closely about me during my morning trysts with God at sunrise. Yes, the weather had changed for the better, but the only change I saw in my audiences was a growing antagonism to the message. Josiah's work for God was having an effect – but the effect was negative, and I was the one who was feeling it. Being a prophet was beginning to feel less and less safe. Had I not been given God's assurance of protection, I would have been very worried.

Few people in Jerusalem could have failed to hear Yahweh's words by now, and many visitors from the country had also filled the audiences. Travellers from the northern areas were common, recognisable by their cosmopolitan approach to many things in which we of Judah were more conservative. It showed first in their clothing and hair styles, but also in their dismissive attitude to the temple of God, which we in Judah rated so highly – at least in theory.

One evening I was in the scroll room of our home as usual, continuing my daily reading of scriptures, with the scroll of Isaiah spread out before me. Nearing the end of his prophecy, I had come across the words:

> "Whom are you mocking?
> Against whom do you open your mouth wide
> and stick out your tongue?
> Are you not children of transgression,
> the offspring of deceit,
> you who burn with lust among the oaks,
> under every green tree,
> who slaughter your children in the valleys,
> under the clefts of the rocks?"[122]

Isaiah's message was no different from mine! Just as blunt, just as distressing. Given more than 70 years ago, yet nothing had improved and still no punishment had come. Why?

God had completely destroyed the kingdom of Israel, yet Judah continued. Of course, Israel had been completely wicked, everyone knew that. This was justice. Despite the sins of Judah, as a nation it was clearly better than Israel had been. If the truth were told, I was certain that Judah, my nation, was better than Israel.

As I mused, I noticed that the room seemed to be growing quieter. The night sounds heard through the shutters were fading, and the noise of my family in the other rooms was growing more muffled. By this time, I was wondering what was going on and stood up suddenly, knocking over my stool. No sound. Hitting the floor, the stool had bounced a little and

---

[122] Isaiah 57:4-5

rolled, but I had heard no sound. I have to laugh now as I recall it, because it seems so strange that I should have had no idea what was happening. Again, it was the presence of God, but it was different. Slower. Not so profoundly or irresistibly satisfying. Maybe it was the tenor of my thoughts that made the difference – proud thoughts are never attractive to God.

Whatever the reason, my growing awareness of Yahweh's presence that night did not bring with it the same terrified yet happy excitement as before. External sounds seemed to disappear completely. Complete stillness reigned, and the room seemed just a little brighter. I finally recognised God as the author of this completely new experience. Deep uncertainty followed: Silence; Waiting. On this occasion, I had time to think while in the presence of God. Time to examine myself and become more aware of the purity and holiness of this all-pervading silence that had filled the room. Contrast and similarity: these were the two concepts that filled my mind, painting a scene of conflict and suffering. Petty pride and self-righteous comparisons were the foundation of the contrast: separating, isolating, estranging me from Yahweh. The similarity was more tenuous, ethereal, diaphanous; a love of purity and holiness. While the presence lasted, it inspired and encouraged me to feel that I really could achieve such purity and holiness and could overcome. I know this description can never hope to do justice to the hand of God, my shepherd. Rather, I hope you will have the opportunity to feel the encouraging hand of Yahweh yourself.

After an unknown length of time spent with the hand of God on me, the room seemed to become a little brighter still. Silence continued to blanket everything, but suddenly, I felt, within, the flame I had come to recognise as the voice of God:

"Have you seen what she did, that faithless one, Israel,
how she went up on every high hill and under every green tree,
and there played the whore?
And I thought,
'After she has done all this she will return to me,'
but she did not return,
and her treacherous sister Judah saw it.
She saw that for all the adulteries of that faithless one, Israel,

> I had sent her away with a decree of divorce.
> Yet her treacherous sister Judah did not fear,
> but she too went and played the whore.
> Because she took her whoredom lightly, she polluted the land,
> committing adultery with stone and tree.
> Yet for all this her treacherous sister Judah did not return to me
> with her whole heart, but in pretence,
> declares the Lord."[123]

Could I hear the words? I'm still not sure. As previously, I could see the words in my mind, written in fiery letters. But could I also hear them? I think so, but there was such an overarching silence in the room that it felt like an almost silent whisper. These are some of the details I remember now, but at the time it was the words that filled my mind and body and completely claimed my attention. It was obvious that these words were in response to my thoughts about the idol worship condemned by Isaiah. My reflections, so critical of the sins of Israel, had whitewashed the sins of Judah. God's words continued to show me my error:

> "Faithless Israel has shown herself more righteous
> than treacherous Judah."[124]

Impossible! Everyone knew that Judah was better than Israel! My response was one of complete and utter denial. God's words simply could not be right… could they?

God's words have always stayed imprinted on my mind. All are present for me to read whenever I choose, but some stand out more than others, shining with a greater brightness. And of all the words that God has ever spoken to me, these words have burned particularly brightly, flaring up to white-hot brilliance from time to time. When I heard that Jehoiakim had murdered a prophet – my friend – these words burned fiercely, outshining any of the messages of hope written alongside. As I watched Jerusalem burn, saw God's temple crumble to ash, and sorrowed as the hapless corpses of thousands were consumed in the bonfires of Topheth, this sentence flamed like a torch

---

[123] Jeremiah 3:6-10
[124] Jeremiah 3:11

within me. Many, many times during my career as a prophet, their brightness has been a mute reminder of the dangers of self-satisfaction and comparisons of ourselves with others.

Complete disorientation came with the next words: ungentle, wrenching, dislocating.

"Go, and proclaim these words toward the north, and say,
'Return, faithless Israel,
declares the Lord.
I will not look on you in anger, for I am merciful,
declares the Lord;
I will not be angry forever.' "[125]

"The north." "Go." My first foreign assignment, and I was not ready for it. "Too young. Too young. I'm just not old enough. Someone else would do it better." The words kept repeating in my mind and I didn't seem to be able to stop them.

Apparently Judah had heard enough of my message. Yet, frustrated though I was with the stubborn, stony hearts of my people in Jerusalem, at least I felt at home there. Yahweh now wanted me to stop telling Jerusalem and shift my focus to Israel. The people of Jerusalem had been warned, and now Israel must hear a new message from God – a message of hope.

℞

Preparation for travel is not difficult when all you really need is your voice.

Informing my parents was the most difficult task, and this was accomplished early the next morning. Azariah was listening and immediately expressed his opinion that the whole proposal was ridiculous and that my parents must obviously refuse their consent to such a hare-brained scheme.

My statement that this was God's instruction meant nothing to Azariah. He positively did not believe me.

My mother and father let their perplexity show for a while, but in this case, my father was led by my mother. Although no-

---

[125] Jeremiah 3:12

one had heard any noise from the scroll room last night, my mother believed my report and for her, that concluded the discussion. After a question or two to make sure she understood as much of the detail as I could explain, she bustled about making sure that I would have what I needed. A bag for the journey with some spare items of clothing, some money to carry in my belt and other things she considered essential. Her bustle and busy-ness presupposed my father's agreement and he didn't argue.

Yet again, facing up confidently to possible opposition had made the opposition melt. At least I could follow this unexpected directive from God with my parents' permission, if not their explicit approval.

Within an hour of finishing breakfast, I was ready to leave, having told my parents what my plans were. Another early morning spent with the rising sun had given me time to make plans. As the shining sliver grew to a flaming disk, highlighting, with an ever-moving play of colours, the delicate swirls of cloud in the heavens, I had considered my way: possible destinations, durations and target audiences. In the presence of Yahweh, ideas had flowed and the conclusions seemed so completely wonderful that I was a little overcome with awe.

Yet the fact was, I didn't really know even so much as the names of some of the places I was to visit! Israel was a foreign land to me – priests of Yahweh had not been very welcome there since the time of Jeroboam, the son of Nebat. Never during my childhood had my parents taken me to the northern kingdom, devastated as it had been by the Assyrians almost one hundred years before. My knowledge of its cities and towns was very limited, and even the towns I had heard of meant nothing to me as places.

But I had a plan, and I knew some places to ask for, so that was enough for today.

As well as the items my mother had packed for me, my bag for the journey included pen and ink and the scroll on which all of God's earlier words to me had been written. Last evening's words were not yet recorded, but I was sure that an opportunity would arise when a rest from walking would allow me time to write.   One fact made me particularly happy: Isaiah was coming with me! My father had given me permission to take the old, but smelly, scroll, and I appreciated his generosity. That smelly scroll would keep me company and hold God's word close to me in the mostly pagan land beyond the borders of Judah.

℞

It was still quite early when I walked hopefully out of the house and took the road that led up over the top of the hill of Anathoth and on to the north. Exchanging a perfunctory "Shalom" with each neighbour or relative I met, I passed out of the town without anyone enquiring why I carried a bag or what business I had in the north. Nor did I volunteer the information, as my mission was not entirely clear in my own mind yet. It seemed easier to avoid questions that I might not have an answer for.

Last night, the words of God had continued. The profound silence had continued to envelop the room and the light filled its furthest recesses, but the presence of God was much more intimate – once I had accepted that Judah truly was worse than Israel had ever been. This acceptance did not come easily, and the struggle in my mind was fierce. In the end, I think it was my new familiarity with the words of Isaiah and Amos that made the difference. These highlighted the fact that God had condemned the same behaviours in each nation and given warnings of coming destruction to both. And now, the evil of Judah had been growing like a vigorous but poisonous weed for almost all of the last one hundred years. Manasseh himself had reigned for more than half of this time, and his relentless pursuit of evil had taken Judah to a very low ebb, beyond the lowest level ever set by Israel.

Throughout my reverie, God had been patient with me and waited – his presence seeming to help my understanding. But with that understanding had come increased worry. Judah – worse than Israel! Israel as a nation was gone. What of Judah? Could the tide be turned, the flood reversed, the river of evil diverted? Was national repentance actually possible for Judah – even with King Josiah in command?

And now I was leaving Judah, and the work God had planned for me would take some time. A sudden thought took away all my hopefulness and left a leaden feeling in my stomach: would Judah still be a kingdom when I returned?

There was so much I had not thought of in my packing, simple matters which later became second nature in my travels. Some evidence of who you are is always helpful; I had none. Careful secreting of any money that won't be needed immediately is advisable – there are many robbers on the roads. All my money was in my belt. I would be travelling alone, with no experience of travelling, no particular vocational skills, and none of the caution or easy confidence that seems to come with age. Although I didn't realise it, I would surely need God's care.

Summer always brings the blazing sun to the hills of Judea. In Anathoth, the next month would be the hottest time of the year, and I would miss this time of growth and maturation. Spring had gone, and with it any expectation of rain for several months. Having made the connection between God's observations about withholding rain and the notable absence of the latter rains, I had also been alert to the lack of growth that spring. A dry spring had been followed in early summer by a time of hot, drying winds. By now, the early figs and grapes should have been ready to harvest, but the figs were few in number, and the grapes small and hard. Already, the scattered sheep on the rocky hills were having difficulty finding their much-needed grass. Already, the hills were the bare brown of late summer. Already, the valleys were dry, the stunted, thirsty plants unable to find the lingering moisture on which they thrive. Conditions were not promising for farmers, shepherds or anyone else. Food would soon become scarce.

The road was dry and dusty, as you might expect, but its raised surface was in reasonable condition, quite smooth and even, with none of the deep potholes and erosion normally found in the local beaten earth roads.

It wasn't long before I met a unit of Judah's army, marching down from the north towards Jerusalem. King Josiah's men, hurrying back to the capital – possibly concluding a term of duty on the border and looking forward to some home leave with their families. The king needed roads on which troops could move quickly, even in wet weather, so roads like this were constructed and maintained by the king's workmen. Traders with their donkeys, and weary pilgrims on foot also used them, confident that the frequent military traffic would keep thieves away. Two such highways headed north from Jerusalem, one travelling almost directly north, and the other – the one I was walking on – passing through Anathoth before turning in a more northerly direction over the hilly terrain. This was the continuation of the road I normally trod between Anathoth and Jerusalem, although there were other, smaller, less direct tracks that I used when seeking solitude.

After an hour or two of walking, the highway had led me to areas I no longer recognised, and it continued to get hotter as I walked on. The heat of the day found me nearing the border with Israel, and I stopped for a while under an olive tree to eat the cake of figs I had brought with me and rest a while. But first, I had to write down the words God had spoken to me last night. The scroll was in my bag, with the pen and ink carefully packed to avoid damage or spilling. Finding a convenient rock on which I could both sit and spread out the scroll in front of me, I wrote out the words of God. Having re-read them a couple of times and fixed some minor mistakes in my writing, I packed them away and enjoyed the figs.

No-one passed as I sat beside the road, alternately dozing and waking. Everyone was waiting for the worst of the heat to pass before continuing their journey in the cool of the day. My plan was to reach Bethel before dark and find a place to stay. First, however, I must cross the border. Movement between the two countries had become quite free and easy, with neither wanting to cause trouble. The Assyrians were busy maintaining a vast, but contracting, empire, and had no wish to pick fights on their peaceful borders. Josiah was content that this was to his advantage, and did not risk the peace through any officious or aggressive behaviour.

ᚳ

Back on the road, I met a trader with two heavily laden donkeys, heading towards Jerusalem. He was anxious to hear of any signs of robbers on the way, but I had seen none. I was equally eager to ask about guards ahead.

"None on the road," he reassured me, "but there is a watch post for each country, one on either side of the road – trying to look inconspicuous." He laughed as he described the two opposing sets of soldiers, carefully placed a short distance apart on opposite sides of the highway, trying to guard their territory while appearing blithely unconcerned. Laughing even louder, he spoke of the dilapidated state of the road between the two guard posts, where he said the potholes were "so big that I almost lost my donkeys in one of them!" Quickly becoming serious, however, he warned, "Make sure you don't do anything unexpected while you are between those guard posts, young man. If you do anything suspicious, they'll be on you as quick as lightning."

Within a few minutes, I had passed the guard posts. I walked unhindered across the de facto border and made my way into Israel. My upbringing was shouting within me that this was entering the land of the pagans, the land of religious traitors and sinners. It was still hard to reconcile this with the words of God, "Faithless Israel has shown herself more righteous than treacherous Judah."[126] No praise for either nation, but a slightly lesser condemnation for Israel. Maybe I would be safer in Israel than in Judah!

My new task had begun.

---

[126] Jeremiah 3:11

Chapter 15

Surprises in Bethel

At first, nothing seemed very different. Possibly the road was not so well maintained, but little else indicated that I was now in a different kingdom.

In little more than twenty years, the empire of Assyria would finally collapse and the power of Babylon would come to fill the void, but even at this time, Assyria had little energy to spare on Israel. Already, there were few soldiers of the overlords to be seen – most of the security in Israel was provided by locally organised militias with limited tactical or monetary support from Assyria.

Travellers were still common, and most were wearing clothes very similar to my own simple tunic and dusty sandals. For poor country folk in both the north and the south it was almost a uniform – they could afford nothing else. This was the clothing I had chosen to wear.

However, as I continued to walk, the differences became more apparent. The road grew worse and travellers seemed less inclined to chat. It was fast approaching sunset and I knew

I should be nearing Bethel. Earlier, a traveller had warned me to look out for a track leading away from the highway around the corner of a hill, saying that the town itself could not be seen from the junction.

With little of the sun still visible above the horizon, I finally came to a place which fitted the description. Fortunately, some residents of Bethel returning from a journey to the north arrived at the intersection at the same time, and reassured me that this was indeed the path to Bethel. Relieved, I climbed with them to the city gates, and we were able to enter together as the guards were preparing to close the gates for the night.

They watched us as we entered, but seemed more interested in preparing their evening meal than in asking us any questions. I was able to walk into the city without saying a word – for which I was grateful, since only a very few words would have been needed for my accent to show that I came from the south. When it came to the local authorities, anonymity was best, for tonight at least.

Dusk had fallen, and I needed to find somewhere to stay for the night. The warmth of summer made the open square near the gate one possible option, but I preferred to find an inn if I could. There were many stories of unpleasant things happening to travellers who stayed in town squares, and I knew nothing about Bethel. Asking a few questions of the helpful strangers with whom I had entered gained me the information that there were several inns in the street directly across the square from the gate. Not only that, but they would take me to the inn they would recommend – clean and safe, they said, and the food exquisite.

We walked across the busy square and entered an equally busy laneway. Private houses, shops and inns stood together cheek by jowl, bordering the dimly lit thoroughfare. My guides stopped outside a building, and one of them, a young man of middling height with a ready smile, led me through the door. His smile was exercised immediately as he spoke to a young woman standing at a clay oven near the entrance. She was flushed with the heat of the cooking and looked flustered, as if we were not the first to interrupt her culinary exercises. "Is your mother around, Maacah?"

"She is just showing a guest to his room. She should be back directly." The girl deftly lifted the clay pot from the flames and placed it on the floor. Another pot scooped up from the floor swiftly took its place on the fire. The smell in the room was delicious, and I hoped there would be room for me to stay in this inn – as long as I could get some of that food!

After a short while, a plump woman entered the room, carrying a cleaning cloth over her arm and breathing heavily. "Maacah, my dear," she puffed, "we really should find a house with no stairs." Another smile lit up the face of my guide, and it struck me that I did not even know his name.

Unwittingly, Maacah provided the information immediately: "Mother, Shobai was wanting to see you."

"Ah, Shobai," wheezed her mother, "I didn't see you there, what with all that running up and down stairs – it's enough to wear a body out. What do you want?"

My friendly acquaintance's ready smile flashed out again as he said, "This traveller needs somewhere safe to stay tonight, Miriam, so I recommended your place – though if I don't leave soon, I'll be staying and having some of that food myself." Miriam and Maacah laughed, while Shobai turned to me and said, "We were in such a hurry to get into the city before the gates closed that we haven't exchanged names yet. My name is Shobai."

"And mine is Jeremiah," I answered.

"Where are you from?" he enquired.

"Anathoth, in Benjamin."

He whistled. "The town of priests?"

"Yes," I said, "and I am from a family of priests." Strangely, it seemed completely reasonable to trust these people, chance met near dark on a foreign road, and in a stuffy kitchen in Bethel, the long-established centre of idol worship in Israel.

"What brings you to Bethel?" asked Miriam.

CR

Singing awoke me from a fitful slumber. I rolled over on my sleeping mat, sat up and sleepily looked around the darkened room. I was in a dormitory-style room with three other men, nearest the door as I had been the last to arrive. The others were still clinging to their sleep in the blacker recesses of the room. Gradually, my sleepiness receded and I began to notice the words of the singer. Wonder of wonders, they were the words of a psalm of King David:

> "This is the day that the Lord has made;
> let us rejoice and be glad in it."[127]

Mellifluous and gentle, clear and melodious, the warm, rich voice continued with the words of the psalm. Sweet melody indeed.

> "You are my God, and I will give thanks to you;
>
> you are my God; I will extol you.
>
> Oh give thanks to the Lord, for he is good;
>
> for his steadfast love endures forever!"[128]

The last sentence was sung with just the right balance of vibrant joy and respectful admiration, and I wondered if the singer had stood still for those words, as we always did in the south, concentrating on the rising tide of thankfulness so beautifully expressed by David. As those last triumphant words came to an end, it was as if the entire world had been holding its breath and now tumbled over itself in noise.

Voices called for water. Pans clashed and rang discordantly. The moment was lost and the world rushed headlong into another day, seeming eager to overtake the acknowledgement of God and rush ahead on its own.

Who was the singer? And why were the words of David being sung so beautifully in this bastion of wickedness? Rising

---

[127] Psalm 118:24
[128] Psalm 118:28-29

to my feet – a little stiffly after the long walk of the day before – I quickly rolled up my mat and cloak and put them in my bag. Across the doorway hung a plain brown woven curtain, which I pushed aside silently. Passing into the short passageway beyond, I walked past two other doorways with similar brown curtains that provided privacy for the other patrons of this surprising inn.

Last night had delivered some new acquaintances who could well become friends. When Shobai had asked my reason for visiting Bethel, there was a strong temptation to answer in vague and noncommittal terms, but God had been showing me that facing up to things straight away was normally the best way to work. Since I had come to bring God's message to Bethel, why not start delivering it now? Learning this lesson – "do it now" – has been very important for my work. It isn't always easy.

Miriam and Maacah had also seemed interested to hear about my background, so I explained that I had come as a messenger of God – "Yahweh, the God of Israel," I added, just to make sure they knew who I meant. They knew, alright. As I gave my short explanation, they had exchanged glances and a look of eagerness had come into their eyes. I had stopped, a little puzzled and struggling to understand their responses.

Shobai had seen me looking uncertain and reassured me, "You don't need to worry, Jeremiah," he said. "We are all excited to hear what you say. Miriam here has been a worshipper of God all her life," then with a grin, "and that's a very long time!" He had artfully dodged the cloth she flicked at him, and continued. "In fact, she is the one who convinced me about Yahweh our God."

"And Maacah?" I had asked, looking towards her.

Simply expressed, but clearly heartfelt, was her answer: "I worship Yahweh, the God of Israel."

Unfortunately, that had been the end of our discussion. At that moment a group of hungry guests had entered the kitchen and demanded a meal. There had been no further opportunity for private speech with any of the trio, and Shobai had left soon afterward. A delectable meal had followed, and Maacah's cooking skills were still being lauded by all as I wiped the last of the vegetable stew from my plate with a piece of delicious bread.

My memories of that meal were still fresh as I entered the room in which we had eaten the previous evening. No-one was in the room except Maacah. Busily laying out serves of bread and dried fruit on tables, she was getting the room ready for the guests who would soon start to trickle in from their beds.

"Was that you singing before?" I asked.

"Yes," she said, turning towards me a little awkwardly.

"You sing beautifully," I said, admiringly. She looked embarrassed and turned back to the table, making a minute adjustment to a bowl of new figs. "Do you know where the words come from?" I continued.

"My mother told me that they came from a psalm of King David," she replied, without turning around, still putting the finishing touches to the arrangements on the tables. "It is my favourite song. Anyway, I must go."

With that, she turned and walked through the doorway into the kitchen area. I watched her go: she was slim and attractive – and she believed in God also. Not at all what I had expected to find in Bethel!

℈

As I ate my sumptuous breakfast, I pondered my next course of action. Other travellers had found their way into the dining room by this time, and we ate together amid a drone of varied voices and frequent praises of the food. Inns are normally noted for providing only very basic fare, but this inn was clearly an exception. Differing accents proclaimed different origins, and I looked around at my fellow travellers, wondering what brought each to the town. Was it religion, or trade, or was it family ties?

It was in the towns and cities that I had expected to see the more outlandish attire brought by distant travel and the fashions of the rich. Many of these could already be seen in

Jerusalem, even amongst my own relatives. The evening meal had not left me disappointed.

However, what I found strangest were the silly hairstyles! Even within Judah, as I had walked north, the common hairstyles had changed. There were more with trimmed beards, more with hair clipped into funny shapes, and overall, it seemed to me that there was a greater concentration on personal appearance. I knew that some styles had their basis in religious worship, but others? Why would people want to look like that? I had no idea how men could manage to wave their hair and frizz the ends of it so much, but frizz it they did and the results were sometimes laughable. Nevertheless, these hairstyles had their origin in Assyria, and one has to be rather careful to avoid laughing at the overlords. I was careful.

In the years since that day, I have seen far more absurd hairdos, but at that time I was quite ignorant of the lengths to which people will go to make themselves "beautiful" – and how many hours can be spent in such endeavours!

Maacah continued to bustle in and out, providing extra food and pouring wine for the thirsty. She obviously didn't spend hours trying to copy extravagant hairstyles, but her long flowing hair was clearly not neglected either and, despite being modestly covered, its lustrous waves drew many an admiring glance from the men in the assembled company.

❧

Breakfast had finished, and I was walking through the dining area with my bag in readiness to leave when Shobai, my acquaintance of the previous evening, appeared. He carried a key across his shoulder, and he seemed to be looking for someone. When he saw me, his ready smile lit up his face.

"I was hoping you wouldn't have gone yet," he said. "Can you come to my home and talk?"

Another coincidence? Another blessing!

"Yes, I can," I answered, and gave him a smile of my own. My friends and family have always tried to convince me to smile more. They say I am mostly too serious, but I don't find it hard to smile when I am with people I trust. As my work for God has won me more and more enemies in life, it has become harder to find anyone I can trust. But Shobai was never hard to trust, nor did he ever let me down.

After paying for my stay at Miriam's inn – the food alone would have been well worth the cost – I walked with Shobai to his house. As we walked, he asked me more about my background. Needing to explain who I was brought one of my internal struggles to a head. Should I explain who my father was? In my opinion, announcing myself as the son of the High Priest was boasting and revelling in human importance. Had the worship of Yahweh in Judah and Israel been complete and genuine, my feelings might well have been different, but announcing myself as a messenger of Yahweh and then promoting myself as the son of the leader of an establishment which God condemned so heartily – this did not seem right. So I told Shobai that I was the son of Hilkiah, one of the priests in Anathoth[129], a description I have used consistently ever since.

As we walked up the hill from Miriam's inn, we came to an open area, with a raised section in the centre. This, Shobai told me, was the high place where Jeroboam the son of Nebat had put his famous golden calf. Of course, the calf itself was no longer there – the gold had been much too attractive to the conquering Assyrians – but the altar remained. A carved Asherah pole brooded over the site and as we passed by, many worshippers were in various stages of paying their respects to their goddess.

I gazed with fascination at the ritual landscape laid out before me. This, then, was the geographic centre of idolatry in Israel, the honey pot of paganism. Whatever else it may have been, this place was certainly popular, its altars busy with offerings.

Shobai guided me past the misled but adoring crowds, and we descended a couple of streets from the high place before stopping outside a house. I was not used to seeing private

---

[129] Jeremiah 1:1

houses with locked doors – in Anathoth we didn't see a need – but I had noticed that many of the doors in Bethel seemed to have keyholes in them and many of those walking through the streets were carrying keys just as Shobai was. At least his was of a newer, smaller style than I had seen before, less than a cubit in length and not looking very heavy at all. Still, it would be annoying to feel the need to carry a key with you everywhere! Taking the key from his shoulder, Shobai pushed it through the hole at the side of the door and followed it with his entire hand and arm. Almost immediately, the door swung inward. I was intrigued, but we had not come to talk about locks, so I swallowed my questions and went inside.

When in Bethel, Shobai lived with his aged father and mother, but most of his time was spent working their ancestral lands a little to the north. Shobai's older brother farmed the land full time, while Shobai often sold the produce in Bethel or other nearby towns. He had been returning from such a trading trip when I had met him the previous night, having successfully and profitably sold the last of their stock of premium early figs. As a special delicacy, the early figs could normally be relied on to make a significant contribution to the family income, and this year was no exception. Apparently, there had been no shortage of spring rain around Bethel. Coincidence? Or a fulfilment of God's prophecies? However, God had not given me any special information about the weather in Israel, so I couldn't draw any conclusion. It was just another thing to make a mental note of.

Over the last 40 years I have met many people from Israel as part of my job as a prophet to the nations, and Shobai's parents were quite typical. Yahweh was their God and they worshipped him consistently, but they also worshipped Baal, Asherah and any other gods that might take their fancy. There were many gods on offer, presented to them by the people of other nations whom the Assyrians had brought into the land. Feast days for many idols would find them sharing the sober religious attentions paid to the appropriate god, offering the specified offerings and joining in the revelling which always followed. There was nothing exclusive in their worship and no feeling that there should be. They believed that they could serve Yahweh while also serving a multitude of other gods. But Yahweh is a jealous God. Many who try to serve him in this way do not realise that it is not possible to serve Yahweh and any other god. Shared worship is simply not worship at all[130].

Shobai already recognised this to some extent, and the subject of exclusive worship came up several times as we sat talking to his parents that morning. It was obviously important to him that the gods of the nations brought in by the Assyrians should be rejected, but I wasn't sure that he was so convinced about the idols that had been around in Israel for centuries. I helped him as best I could with the words of God from our scriptures, but none of the words seemed to make any impression on his parents. They were perfectly happy with their religion. Any suggestion that their worship did not meet the requirements of the God they were trying to worship rolled off them like water off a duck's back.

Our discussion was friendly enough and lasted quite some time, and my understanding of how people think was broadened more than you might expect from an hour's polite conversation. As a young man who had not travelled widely and had grown up in a wealthy home where outward expressions of complete dedication to God were the norm, this open acknowledgement of religion as an adjustable convenience was a surprise to me. Yet when I pondered on it later that night, I felt that maybe the openness was the only real difference.

My family would never have acknowledged any God but Yahweh, but the life my father lived seemed more like one of quiet cooperation or appeasement than an outstanding act of faithful leadership. He did not want to upset anyone. With Josiah as king, that meant cooperation with godliness. But what would it mean if Josiah was to be replaced with a king whose mind leaned towards idolatry? What if one of Josiah's young sons became king? Prince Jehoiakim was already six years old – not much younger than Josiah had been when he had become king – but he showed no signs of the godliness his father had reportedly shown at such an age. The inhabitants of Jerusalem

---

[130] Exodus 34:13-14

knew Jehoiakim as a malicious and spiteful boy, already showing many of the signs of evil which would characterise his later reign as king. How would my father or my brother Azariah respond to the pressures of a king such as Jehoiakim might become?

I didn't want to think any further along that line. All I could do was to hope that Josiah would live a long and fruitful life, convincing his nation to be true to Yahweh their God.

After an hour or so, Shobai's parents left to buy food from the market and we were free to talk. But the day was slipping away and I was eager to begin my work in the north. Yet again, I had the conviction that it wouldn't get easier if I waited.

"What are your plans, Jeremiah?" asked Shobai.

"To speak the words of Yahweh to those living in the area of Israel," I answered.

"How?"

"I have been prophesying in Jerusalem for three months by simply going to different places, finding somewhere to stand, and speaking," I explained. "Some people listen, most ignore me, some would like to hurt me."

"Israel might be different from Jerusalem," Shobai warned.

"God said he would look after me as long as I don't let my opponents stop me, Shobai," was my confident answer. While that experience in Topheth still niggled – cuts and bruises weren't quite the level of protection I had expected – I supposed it wasn't too bad, compared with what I had read of happening to other prophets.

"Are you sure?" Shobai looked doubtful.

"God promised," I replied, simply.

"Oh, I see," he said slowly, then continued; "Will you be working only in Bethel?"

"No," I replied. "I have a few other places to go, although I don't know much about any of them."

My experience of being a prophet is that everyone you speak to expects you to know exactly what you are doing and what will happen next, as well as how soon and why. However, most of the time God's instructions to me have been specific in some details, but completely silent in others. There was the time when God sent me to prophesy and told me exactly where to go, what to say and what to do. What he didn't mention was that afterwards I would be seized and beaten.... Certainly it was better not to have known in advance, but that just reflects the level of foreknowledge I have as a prophet: it varies. Before I had come to Israel, the Lord Yahweh had helped me to build a list of places to go and some things to do. While developing my itinerary that morning, I had marvelled at the planning behind it. It had seemed wonderful – even to me with so little knowledge of Israel. But now that I was about to start the actual work, I could see all the gaps in my knowledge. Maybe God was going to give me more information as I went along, but at the moment, I felt very ill-equipped for the job.

Chapter 16

"Return, Faithless Israel"

It was almost noon before I began speaking to the people of the north, standing near the gate of Bethel.

Shobai had been a great help to me that morning, and I felt that in him I had found a good friend. He was a few years older than me, but had a thirst for the knowledge of God that I had not met in Judah. We had talked for quite a long time about Yahweh and his plans. When he heard that I was to deliver a message calling on Israel to return to Yahweh, he was eager to ask what God wanted of him, personally. By this time, I felt that I understood what God wanted most from his people. Faithfulness – exclusive faithfulness – like that which a wife or husband promises to give to their spouse. Some people have said to me that this is a bad example because a man can quite legally have several wives. It is true that God only compares the sinful behaviour of his people with the behaviour of an unfaithful wife or a prostitute, not an unfaithful husband. Possibly that reflects the fact that, while we allow men to have more than one wife, we have never allowed a woman to have more than one husband. Maybe that is somehow "natural" and I am the one who is wrong, but it doesn't seem to me that this was how God made it in the beginning with Adam and Eve. One man, one woman.

Shobai had been a little shocked by this demand for exclusive worship of Yahweh, but gradually seemed to become more convinced as I showed him various words from my treasured scroll of Isaiah where God shows himself to be a jealous God – just like a jealous husband. He said he would have to make some changes in his own life and see whether he could get his family to make them in theirs. If only the people of Judah had responded like this – even one of them!

Now I would find out whether anyone else would respond. My voice, speaking the words of Yahweh, rang out over the noises of the market at the gate of Bethel. It was still not a beautiful voice, but I had learned some tricks over the last three months while prophesying in Jerusalem. I had learned to make my voice carry more so that people could hear me from further away. I couldn't describe what the difference was in how I spoke, but it worked.

Everyone within earshot froze as I spoke the first words of Yahweh:

> "Return, faithless Israel,
> declares the Lord.
> I will not look on you in anger, for I am merciful,
> declares the Lord;
> I will not be angry forever."[131]

There was no doubt about it, people were paying more attention than they ever had in Judah. Why?

September, 626BC

Three months later, I was back in Bethel again.

I had spent a week in Bethel initially, and there was no doubt about it: people were listening. There wasn't any

---

[131] Jeremiah 3:12

wholesale repentance of the city, or anything like it, but at least some were listening. On one occasion, the crowd had even cheered as I spoke!

Since then, I had followed the path God had laid out for me the morning I had left Anathoth, travelling through many places in the north of Israel. From Samaria I had sent a letter south, and now I was back in Bethel, as my letter had said I would be.

Through Ephraim, Manasseh, Simeon, and even up north into Naphtali, I had walked the dusty roads of Israel, and the inhabitants had all welcomed me, and, to some extent, God's message. The call to repentance seemed to have struck a chord with some, and I had felt some optimism as I walked back towards Bethel.

The northern areas of Israel were in a terrible state. Some cities had been restored after the destruction of the Assyrian invasion, but many towns and villages were still in ruins almost a century later[132]. Those who lived in the area were very poor, and there was no spare money or time for repairs or new construction. Life was a hand-to-mouth existence. Taxes were high, and there was no feeling of community. People from many different lands had been settled next to each other by the Assyrians, but language, culture and religion were all major stumbling blocks. It was as if there were many individual ghettos everywhere, each quite insular, and each a little cautious about upsetting anyone else. Trouble seemed rare, but so did happiness. Shobai's easy and frequent smile was quite unusual.

There were no magnificent altars or idols, but there were many simple altars on the high places, and the worship of Yahweh was freely mixed with the worship of idols. Now, however, God's call for repentance was finding some response. If only the people would answer the call, repentance would bring success and happiness as it always has. Maybe then society could recover. However, I had no idea what should be done with all of the imported foreigners who were now spread

---

[132] 2 Chronicles 34:6

over the centre of the land, particularly around Samaria. They simply weren't Hebrews, and God had given the land to his people. What should we do?

Shobai had travelled with me to Shiloh and Shechem. Shiloh was the first place in Israel where Yahweh had put his name, but now it was a ruin[133]. Almost no-one lived there, and the site where the tabernacle had stood was overgrown and unused, its surrounding walls broken down and decrepit.

This was how God treated even his chosen places if his people did not worship him. Would he do the same to Jerusalem? At that time, I didn't know the answer, but found it hard to imagine Jerusalem ruined, overgrown and empty. The people of Bethel had been willing to listen, and this had brought back some hope. I was optimistic that Josiah could win the day, and re-establish the worship of God in Judah and Israel. But I was reckoning without the relentless determination of people everywhere to tear down all restraint and pursue a path of endless self-indulgence. Already, Jerusalem was doomed; fortunately, though, I didn't realise it.

It seems that God had wanted me to see the ruins of Shiloh and to understand its fate. His later messages to me referred to Shiloh a couple of times[134], and having seen the ruins made it easier to explain to the listeners what had happened there. Having had God's name in a place would not magically protect it from attack if true worship was missing. God would only dwell among humans while they tried to worship him his way. Shiloh made a big impression on Shobai. He knew some of the history and could recognise that there had been no shortage of worship when Shiloh had been destroyed, but it had not been worship as God required it. This seemed to help to convince him that he needed to exclude any acceptance or worship of other gods from his own thoughts.

Shechem was mostly a ruin too, but was still quite popular as a market centre, so I delivered God's message to Israel there

---

[133] Joshua 18:1; 19:51; Judges 21:19; 1 Samuel 1:3; Psalm 78:60; Jeremiah 7:12-15
[134] Jeremiah 7:12-15; Jeremiah 26:4-6

also. Some positive responses came and I was able to talk to quite a few people one-to-one, particularly several who knew Shobai. It was at Shechem that I learned the importance of carrying some form of identification, and if Shobai had not been with me and vouched for me, it could have ended quite differently. Standing on a trader's cart, I had just begun speaking God's words to quite a large audience when an Assyrian officer approached with a small group of soldiers at his heels. He let me continue, but was clearly suspicious as he heard me continue with words like:

> "I will take you, one from a city and two from a family,
>   and I will bring you to Zion;"[135]

or

> "At that time Jerusalem shall be called the throne of the Lord,
>   and all nations shall gather to it,
>   to the presence of the Lord in Jerusalem."[136]

Whatever the cause, he stayed until I finished, then immediately approached me.

"Who are you, and where are you from?" he demanded, in Aramaic. When I looked rather blank, he asked the question again in slow and deliberate Hebrew.

"My name is Jeremiah...," I started, when Shobai interrupted, speaking in fluent Aramaic.

"He's a young friend of mine, sir. We came from Shiloh this morning. My name is Shobai and I live near Bethel – when I'm not busy selling our produce." His ready smile lit up his face and he put his arm around my shoulders. To any Israelite, my accent would have been a clear indication that I was not from Shiloh or Bethel, but this officer was not a local, and his accent was much more obvious than mine. The officer was very happy to talk to Shobai, since he could do so in his preferred Aramaic, but he did cast more than one questioning look in my direction. Shobai kept going: speaking very politely, saying "sir" frequently and smiling often, until after a few

---

[135] Jeremiah 3:14
[136] Jeremiah 3:17

minutes the officer let us go without any more trouble. Although not fluent in Aramaic, I was not completely ignorant of it either, and could understand much of what the officer said. He had asked for some evidence of who I was. He wanted no troublemakers in the area. Shobai's Aramaic and winning smile had carried the day.

Being a long way from home, I couldn't fix this deficiency immediately, but from that time on, I always tried to carry some form of introduction or proof of who I was.

After we left Shechem, Shobai returned to his farm and I went on alone, telling people everywhere that God wanted them to acknowledge their sins. For some, this demand was far beyond them: how dare I suggest that they had sinned? But for many others the call was timely, as they saw their nation wallowing in paganism and completely lacking direction. If only the former glory of Israel could be restored, they thought. In villages and ruins, towns and individual homes, the sadness and suffering had prepared the people for something. I hoped it would be repentance and reformation, so I spoke to all I could find. From Bethel in the south up to Galilee in the north, the message of God was heard in the markets and streets. By the time I arrived in Samaria to send my letter, I had already spoken to hundreds of people who were responding to God by acknowledging both that Israel had sinned, and that they personally had sinned.

I had also learnt many lessons in my travels and had good reason to be very grateful for God's loving care each day. Greedy innkeepers had taught me to hide my money until a price was agreed, and only the blessing of God given through a friendly traveller had stopped the cost of that lesson from being much greater than it was. How could I have known that there was no special bed tax in that area? – the innkeeper had made it sound very plausible. Sellers in markets had taught me all the tricks about handling fruit so that its blemishes would not be seen by the purchaser, though there were several times when I went hungry because of bad fruit before I learned the tricks.

Potentially, the most dangerous incident was about a week after Shobai and I had parted. I had been dozing under a tamarisk tree beside the road in the heat of the day, with my back leaning against the gnarled trunk, when a young man of about my own age left the road and looked as if he would like to talk to me. Doing my best to shake the cobwebs from my mind, I sat up straight and greeted him. "Shalom," I said slowly.

The young man looked at me, as if weighing up his options. Even with only that single word, he probably knew that I was no local. Finally, he said, "Shalom. Live nearby?" Looking around he added, "Travelling alone?"

With more experience, I might have left these questions unanswered, but instead I said, "Yes, I'm travelling alone. I'm from Judah."

He looked pleased and asked, "Do you mind if I sit with you under the tree? The sun is shining something fierce today."

I waved my hand in agreement and he sat down near me. As he did so, I caught a glimpse of a blade in the knotted bundle he carried over his shoulder. Of course, it might have been just a small knife such as travellers often carried – I had one myself – but it looked a little larger than that and it put me on my guard. He didn't notice, and continued the conversation as he mopped his brow.

"Hottest day for a while, don't you think?" he asked.

I agreed, briefly, but by then I was rather eager to get away from him.

"My name's Nathan, by the way. Seen any Assyrian soldiers today?" he enquired.

"None." My answer was as brief as I could make it.

"Heard of any robbers at all? I hear it's a lucrative business around here, now that the Assyrians keep away." He looked at me intently, and I wondered what his aim was.

"I'm just passing through," I temporised.

"Ah. Visiting friends up north?"

"No," I said shortly.

Again he looked at me intently, and seemed to make up his mind. "You look like a clever sort," he said. "There's a few of us that work the roads around here, if you know what I mean." I didn't, but let him keep going anyway. This was all getting rather worrying. "You like money don't you?" he continued, but didn't wait for an answer. "Of course you do, everyone likes money," he said, "and we have a good way of making sure that we get our fair share. We all work together, collect the money together and share it out amongst ourselves. How does that sound to you?" he asked, looking eagerly at me for an answer. When I didn't respond immediately, he looked away. "We need another man," he said, confidingly. "Pelet went and got himself killed last week. Too careless with a rich man carrying a dagger. Of course, we killed him afterwards too, but that didn't help poor Pelet." He looked back at me once more, looking a little wistful. He was obviously missing his partner in crime and thought I might make a good replacement.

It was at that stage that I finally noticed another man, standing under a tree on the other side of the road, not moving, but keeping his eyes glued on me. He looked untidy, dirty, armed and dangerous. He wasn't specifically showing off the dagger in his hand or the sword in his waistband, but then, he wasn't bothering to hide them either.

My young confidant saw me looking across the road and nodded. "Oh yes, you've seen Zimri too. We have the place pretty well covered, you know, even if I do say so myself." I wondered how many more of them there were. What should I do?

"You asked me if I like money," I said; "the answer is 'Yes,' as long as it comes honestly."

"Now don't get all high and mighty, my friend," he responded. "We're just evening up the wealth, after all. Those filthy rich fellas don't need all they have anyway, and as long as they hand it over quickly, we let 'em live."

"Well, I won't be a robber, it's evil. God forbids it."

He looked at me uncertainly. Maybe he had never heard anything like that before, but for whatever reason, he suddenly stood up, turned around and walked off, calling out to Zimri as he walked, "Hey Zimri, this bloke's no use, we'll have to try someone else."

Zimri swaggered towards me, and now he *was* showing off his weapons. "We can't just let 'im go like that, Nathan," he said truculently, "he's sure to tell someone;" and he eased his sword out of his waistband.

"Nah, you don't need to worry about him, Zimri. I don't think he's quite all there in the head. He won't be any good for us, but we don't need to worry about him either."

Zimri continued to size me up for a few moments more, then pushed his sword back under his cloak and strutted away down the road. I noticed three others emerging from the shrubbery to meet him a short way down the road and realised more fully the danger I had been in. And possibly still was in. I slowly picked up my pack and walked in the opposite direction, taking care not to look too purposeful or hurried.

Yes, travelling alone can indeed be dangerous, and my three months of travel in Israel had taught me many unexpected lessons.

When I arrived back in Bethel, I heard the confirmation I had hoped for: Josiah was on the way, and due to arrive the very next day.

⊂⊋

There is absolutely no doubt that I should not have been surprised. When God sets things up, they always work.

Following God's instructions, I had sent a messenger from Samaria to deliver a letter to King Josiah reporting on the state of worship in Israel and the positive response that some people were showing to God's call for repentance[137]. The letter had

---

[137] There is no evidence in the Bible of Jeremiah sending such a letter to Josiah, but we know that some time between the twelfth and eighteenth years of his reign, Josiah travelled into Israel. No reason is given. The work he did there fits the description which follows in this chapter.

suggested that he might be welcomed here, doing the same work as he had been doing in Jerusalem, destroying idols and pagan altars. I had signed the letter, "Jeremiah, the son of Hilkiah," and wondered what chance there was that it would ever be delivered.

The messenger had been paid to wait for up to two days for an answer from the king and then to return to Samaria, where I would meet him after one week. It sounds a bit complex, but it worked. Of course.

When I returned to Samaria to meet the messenger I had dispatched, he had a scroll with him, sealed with the seal of Shaphan and written at the command of King Josiah. As I read the letter, I wondered how Shaphan felt about me after that embarrassing interview with Josiah, where the king had expressed his displeasure with Maaseiah and Shaphan for hiding my message from him. However he may have felt, though, it didn't show in this letter, which briefly stated that the king would make the necessary arrangements for a religious visit to the kingdom of Israel at the time suggested.

I'm not sure how King Josiah made those arrangements with the Assyrian leaders, but when I arrived back at the end of the sixth month of the year, Bethel was agog with the news of the coming visit of King Josiah. Back at the inn, I found Miriam and Maacah looking forward excitedly to seeing the young king who had turned to Yahweh so strongly.

When Josiah entered the gates of Bethel it was to a very different reception from that which I had expected. Shobai and I were there to watch, and even Miriam and Maacah came for a short time, leaving the inn unattended while they did so. There was cheering and shouting from the populace, while parading Assyrian soldiers demonstrated the fading splendour of empire. The leaders welcomed this important neighbouring monarch, and Josiah was formally welcomed to Bethel and feted for the rest of the day. Many people had come to Bethel to join in the celebrations, and a feast was held for all the important people.

Naturally, we were not invited, so Shobai and I made our own plans instead. As soon as there was an opportunity, I would make myself known to someone in the king's party. There was sure to be someone I knew among them.

In my letter to King Josiah, I had suggested that he travel north from Bethel to areas where there were fewer Assyrian soldiers and more Israelites who might respond to Yahweh's call.

Towards the end of the day, I went to the grand buildings in which the reception was taking place and spoke to the guards on duty. It took some time, but eventually a message was delivered to the king's attendants and Shaphan came out to meet me.

"Ah, Jeremiah," he said, "you received the king's letter?"

"Yes," I replied. "It filled me with hope."

"Our king is an amazing man," said Shaphan, "and our God blesses his work." Those striking eyes were challenging me, possibly even mocking me a little, but it seemed that he had forgotten or forgiven my interference that had earned him the criticism of the king.

"Yes," I agreed. "But what are his plans from here?"

"Didn't you make some suggestions, trying to lead the king in your way instead of ours – as you see it?" Shaphan's gentle smile took any possible antagonism out of the words, and it was clear that he had forgotten nothing of our previous meetings.

CR

To this day, I still do not know how Josiah achieved it, but we left Bethel the next day, free to travel north with no supervision beyond a small detachment of Assyrian soldiers. And not only that, but these soldiers were all Israelites. The Assyrian army often enlisted soldiers from defeated nations, and quite a few Israelite soldiers had joined the Assyrian army. I'm told that at one time there were even 60 Assyrian chariots in one battle group that were crewed by Israelite charioteers.

Shobai and I said a quick good-bye to Miriam and Maacah. It was to be quite some time before I would meet them again. In some ways it was harder than leaving home had been.

Northward through the towns of Ephraim and Manasseh we went, with the king's men and the Assyrian soldiers providing security and appearing to come to amicable agreements regarding the necessary travel arrangements. To be honest, they seemed to be very willing to greet each other as friends. The soldiers from Israel were quite content to work for the king of Assyria, but they were also very happy to welcome a Hebrew king to their land.

Josiah's progress was slow and careful. He did not want to arouse antagonism, but in a village near the ruins of Shiloh, the situation seemed right to begin the work he had come for, the work for which God had invited him north.

We stopped under a collection of trees in the main street of the village, with market stalls clustered around, and the inevitable altars and idols. I spoke God's words to an audience who had really come to see King Josiah, but were willing to listen to me for a while. Within me the familiar fire burned, but for once, it spread to the audience as well, and the words of God drove them to action:

> "Only acknowledge your guilt,
> that you rebelled against the Lord your God
> and scattered your favours among foreigners
> under every green tree,
> and that you have not obeyed my voice,
> declares the Lord.
> Return, O faithless children,
> declares the Lord;"[138]

As I spoke, two men grasped what God meant when he spoke of Israel scattering her favours among foreigners under every green tree. They were standing one on either side of a small shrine set up against the trunk of a tree, with an idol sitting mute inside, and suddenly they pushed the shrine over. The pottery idol inside tumbled out and one of its arms broke on the ground. One man picked up the arm and waved it over

---

[138] Jeremiah 3:13-14

his head. "Who can worship a god who breaks so easily?" he shouted, and threw the arm against the tree, where it shattered into many pieces. The other man picked up the remainder of the idol and flung it onto the ground, where it too exploded into a hundred pieces.

"These are the gods that have enslaved you," I cried. "Return to the God who gave you freedom from slavery in Egypt. Return to Yahweh, for you have been faithless in worshipping other gods, gods of clay and wood and stone which cannot help you."

As God's words said, there were idols or altars under every green tree, and the crowd enthusiastically tore them all down. Josiah's men also cut down the carved trees shaped to honour Asherah, then finished the work of grinding the idols to powder[139].

During this enthusiastic destruction of idols and altars, the Israelite-Assyrian soldiers looked a little uncertain as to what they should do, but obviously decided finally that it was best to do nothing. This was a local affair. After all, the locals had started the destruction.

℞

This was a wonderful time of genuine religious reformation. King Josiah travelled through many areas of Ephraim, Manasseh, Simeon and Naphtali, through their towns and ruins, tearing down the altars used for sacrifice and incense in the worship of many different gods[140]. Carved Asherah poles and other representations of abhorrent idols all fell before the onslaught of a repentant populace at the word of Yahweh and the encouragement of King Josiah.

And, most wonderful of all, throughout Josiah's entire tour of purification through Israel, the Assyrian soldiers and their overlords did nothing to prevent the wholesale destruction of

---

[139] 2 Chronicles 34:6-7
[140] 2 Chronicles 34:6-7

pagan religious artefacts by a foreign king who had simply come to "visit".

At the most northerly point of our travels through Israel, Yahweh spoke to me. I must continue onward, further north, delivering his messages as a "prophet to the nations." I must leave the next day.

What would happen to the fledgling reformation in Israel? Josiah must return to Judah, and I must travel north. Would the worship of Yahweh revive and soar with renewed strength, or would it falter and die? Individuals must make their own choices. Shobai? Miriam? Maacah? I did my best to encourage Shobai to continue in the truths he had learned from my scroll of Isaiah, and see if he could find any other scrolls of God's word to read. They would help his faith to grow.

And what would happen with my family in Anathoth? Shaphan kindly agreed to pass on to my father a letter which I had quickly written, but would the news of some repentance in Israel have any effect on my family?

ℂℛ

Before continuing my journey northward into Syria, I asked King Josiah for a letter of introduction. He agreed to give it, and the valuable letter was presented to me before we parted. It was written as a general reference, not a specific introduction, since, although I knew only of one immediate task at the time, I remembered my overall job description: "a prophet to the nations." The letter might be needed in other places too. It was.

Below the titles of the king and his seal, it was signed by Shaphan, the secretary.

Continuo

October, 626BC – the 14th year of King Josiah to September, 622BC – the 18th year of King Josiah

My months in Israel were but the start of my work as a prophet to the nations. At various times during the next four years, Yahweh gave me messages to deliver to many nations: to Syria, to Ammon, to Moab, to Edom, to Egypt, to Philistia, to Tyre and Sidon and to many other kingdoms around Judah – even as far afield as Elam. During those years, I spent little time in Anathoth and even less in Jerusalem. Brief visits were all I could spare the time for, and, although I always delivered God's latest messages whenever I was there, it was only in passing. Travel and the day-to-day work of speaking God's message to other nations gave me no time for home.

The capital cities of various nations became familiar to me and their languages stretched my ability to learn. Roads became my daily companions, and I became a seasoned, experienced traveller. In everything God was with me, and in many cities he opened doors to important people in amazing ways. His messages to the nations were accepted with politeness at least. No great national repentance came in any of the nations, but at least I was not beaten, locked up or killed.

I met many diplomats and representatives of rulers, acquaintances I would renew at other times through my ministry. All were remarkably patient and gentle with a very young foreigner, a prophet bringing messages from Yahweh, the God of Israel, a God who was still held in great respect among the nations surrounding Israel. As representatives, they had to be careful of what they said – just as I did – but even so, they seemed more open and genuine about their religious beliefs than the people of Judah ever had.

King Josiah returned to Judah and reigned well. He followed in the footsteps of David, his illustrious ancestor, and gradually took over the reins of government completely, putting his stamp on all areas of the leadership of the kingdom. Gradually he restrained his minders, and gradually he learned more about the underlying religious corruption in his kingdom. Ever so gradually, he started to find out the truth.

The time was coming for his greatest work, his crowning achievement.

Appendix 1

List of Characters

Abigail [1] – wife of **Gemariah [1]** the son of **Hilkiah** and brother of Jeremiah. (Not in the Bible.)

Abigail [2] – wife of **Zaccai**, an official/ruler/noble in the time of King **Josiah**. Welcomed visitors at the Passover in **Josiah**'s eighteenth year. (Not in the Bible.)

Achbor – son of Micaiah. Official/ruler/noble in the time of King Josiah. Sent with **Hilkiah, Ahikam, Shaphan** and **Asaiah** to see **Huldah** the prophetess (2 Kings 22:11-20). Named 'Abdon son of Micah' in 2 Chronicles 34:20. Possibly the father of **Elnathan** mentioned in Jeremiah 26:22 and 36:12.

Ahab – son of Kolaiah. False prophet (with **Zedekiah [2]** the son of Maaseiah (possibly **Maaseiah [2]**)) in captivity. Cursed by God in a letter sent by Jeremiah, with the punishment being that King **Nebuchadnezzar** would roast them in the fire (Jeremiah 29:21-23).

Adaiah – a childhood friend of Jeremiah's who becomes his enemy. (Not in the Bible.)

Ahikam – son of **Shaphan**. Sent with **Hilkiah, Achbor, Shaphan** (probably his father) and **Asaiah** to see **Huldah** the prophetess (2 Kings 22:11-20 and 2 Chronicles 34:19-28). Protected Jeremiah from the people in the time of King **Jehoiakim** (Jeremiah 26:24). Father of **Gedaliah [2]**, the governor appointed by Nebuchadnezzar after the destruction of Jerusalem (Jeremiah 39:14; 40:9 & 11; 41:2; 43:6). See also Jeremiah 39:14.

Amon – son of King **Manasseh** and father of King **Josiah**. An evil king who was 22 years old when he became king and reigned 2 years. Assassinated by his servants (see 2 Kings 21:17-26).

Asaiah – servant of King **Josiah**. Sent with **Achbor, Hilkiah, Ahikam** and **Shaphan** to see **Huldah** the prophetess (2 Kings 22:11-20).

Azariah [1] – Son of **Hilkiah** the High Priest (1 Chronicles 6:13 and Ezra 7:1). High Priest after **Hilkiah**. Father of **Seraiah** who was High Priest at the time of the destruction of Jerusalem (2 Kings 25:18-21). Assumed to be the older brother of Jeremiah.

Azariah [2] – friend of **Daniel** the prophet. Taken into captivity with Daniel in the third/fourth year of King **Jehoiakim**. In Babylon, his name was changed to Abednego.

Azariah [3] – son of Hoshaiah. One of the 'insolent men' who said that Jeremiah was telling a lie when he gave God's answer that the remaining people of Judah should not go to Egypt (Jeremiah 43:2).

Baruch – son of Neriah, son of Mahseiah ('Maaseiah' in KJV, but actually a different name in Hebrew) (Jeremiah 32:12; 51:59). Jeremiah's scribe. Brother of **Seraiah [2]**.

Belibni – a Chaldean officer who looks after Jeremiah on the day when Jerusalem falls. (Not in the Bible.)

Benaiah [1] – son of Kish and a childhood friend of Jeremiah's who becomes his enemy. (Not in the Bible.)

Benaiah [2] – father of **Pelatiah** (Ezekiel 11:1, 13). Son of Kenan and the brother of Kish who was the father of **Benaiah [1]**. A chief man in Anathoth. (No details in the Bible.)

Chelub – a childhood friend of Jeremiah's who becomes his enemy. (Not in the Bible.)

Conaniah – a leader of the Levites with his brothers **Shemaiah [3]** and **Nethanel**. Contributed offerings for the Levites in the great Passover ordered by Josiah in the eighteenth year of his reign (2 Chronicles 35:9).

Coniah – see King **Jeconiah**.

Daniel – the prophet. Writer, under the inspiration of God, of the book of Daniel in the Bible. Probably of noble birth. Taken into captivity by **Nebuchadnezzar** in the third/fourth year of King **Jehoiakim**.

Delaiah [1] – son of Shemaiah (possibly **Shemaiah [1]**, the leader of the Levites in the time of King **Josiah** referred to in 2 Chronicles 35:9). Official of King **Jehoiakim** (Jeremiah 36:12, 25).

Deborah – a neighbour of **Huldah** the prophetess. (Not in the Bible.)

Delaiah [2] – chief servant in **Hilkiah**'s house (in Volume 2). (Not in the Bible.)

Dishon – an Edomite diplomat who visited Jerusalem in the time of Jehoiakim. (Not in the Bible.)

Ebal – an Edomite diplomat who visited Jerusalem in the time of Jehoiakim. (Not in the Bible.)

Ebed-melech – a brave Ethiopian eunuch in King **Zedekiah**'s house. Heard that Jeremiah had been put into a mud-filled cistern by **Shephatiah**, **Gedaliah [1]**, **Jehucal/Jucal** and **Pashhur [2]** (Jeremiah 38:1-6) and asked the king for him to be freed, telling him that the behaviour of his nobles was evil (Jeremiah 38:9). Was given permission to help Jeremiah and took men to lift him out of the cistern (Jeremiah 38:10-13). Given a promise by God that he would be kept safe when Jerusalem was destroyed (Jeremiah 39:15-18).

Eglah – first wife of **Shobai** who died in childbirth. (Not in the Bible.)

Elasah – son of **Shaphan**. Sent by King **Zedekiah [1]** with **Gemariah [1]** the son of **Hilkiah** to **Nebuchadnezzar** in Babylon (Jeremiah 29:3). Carried a letter from Jeremiah to the exiles in Babylon (Jeremiah 29:1-32).

Eliada – a servant in **Hilkiah's** house (in Volume 2). (Not in the Bible.)

Elishama – Secretary to King **Jehoiakim** (Jeremiah 36:12, 20-21).

Elnathan [1] – son of **Achbor**. One of **Jehoiakim**'s nobles. Sent by King **Jehoiakim** with men to fetch **Uriah** the prophet after he fled to Egypt (Jeremiah 26:22). Unsuccessfully urged King **Jehoiakim** not to burn the scroll of Jeremiah's words (Jeremiah 36:12, 25).

Elnathan [2] – of Jerusalem (2 Kings 24:8). Father of Nehushta, the wife of King **Jehoiakim** and mother of King **Jehoiachin**.

Ezekiel – son of Buzi. A priest. Taken into captivity at the same time as King **Jehoiakim**. Writer, under the inspiration of God, of the book of Ezekiel in the Bible.

Gedaliah [1] – son of Pashhur. An official of King **Zedekiah [1]** who, with **Shephatiah** and **Jehucal/Jucal**, asked King **Zedekiah [1]** to kill Jeremiah and then put Jeremiah in the mud-filled cistern (Jeremiah 38:1-6).

Gedaliah [2] – son of **Ahikam**, son of **Shaphan**. Governor appointed by King **Nebuchadnezzar** (Jeremiah 40:5) and subsequently assassinated at Mizpah by **Ishmael** (2 Kings 25:25).

Gemariah [1] – son of **Hilkiah** (Jeremiah 29:3). Assumed to be the son of the High Priest and brother of Jeremiah.

Gemariah [2] – son of **Shaphan** (the secretary). Important official of King **Jehoiakim** (Jeremiah 36:12). Had a chamber in the upper court of the New Gate of the temple (Jeremiah 36:10). Father of **Micaiah** (Jeremiah 36:11).

Hamutal – daughter of Jeremiah of Libnah and wife of King **Josiah**. Mother of King **Jehoahaz** (2 Kings 23:31) and King **Zedekiah [1]** (2 Kings 24:18).

Hananiah [1] – son of Azzur. False prophet. Killed by God in the seventh month of the fourth year of King **Zedekiah** after false prophecies in the fifth month of the same year (Jeremiah 28). Possibly (and assumed in this series to be) the grandfather of **Irijah**, the son of Shelemiah (Jeremiah 37:13). Possibly the brother of **Jaazaniah [3]**.

Hananiah [2] – father of **Zedekiah [3],** an official of King **Jehoiakim** (Jeremiah 36:12).

Hananiah [3] – friend of **Daniel** the prophet. Taken into captivity with Daniel in the third/fourth year of King **Jehoiakim** (Daniel 1:1-2). In Babylon, his name was changed to Shadrach (Daniel 1:6-7).

Hanamel – son of **Shallum [2]** (Jeremiah 32:7). Jeremiah's cousin (Jeremiah 32:8).

Hanamel and Jeremiah's shared paternal uncle – added to provide a house in Jerusalem that could be used by the extended family. There is no evidence in the Bible for the existence of this uncle.

Hashabiah – a leader of the Levites. Contributed offerings for the Levites in the great Passover ordered by King **Josiah** in the eighteenth year of his reign (2 Chronicles 35:9).

Hasshub – son of **Gemariah** [1], Jeremiah's brother. (Not in the Bible.)

Hephzibah – wife of **Azariah** [1] (Jeremiah's brother) and mother of **Seraiah** [3] who was High Priest at the time of the destruction of Jerusalem. (Azariah's wife is not named in the Bible.)

Hilkiah – son of **Shallum** [1] the High Priest (1 Chronicles 6:13). High Priest in the eighteenth year of King **Josiah** (2 Kings 22:3-4). Assumed to be the father of Jeremiah the prophet referred to in Jeremiah 1:1.

Pharaoh **Hophra** – king of Egypt in about the last 2-3 years of the reign of **Zedekiah** and for another 16 years afterwards. Received the people who disobeyed God and left Judah after the destruction of Jerusalem. Jeremiah prophesied against him (Jeremiah 44:30).

Huldah – wife of **Shallum** [3] (2 Kings 22:14). Prophetess. Gave God's answer to the men sent by King **Josiah** after he heard the reading of the Book of the Law.

Irijah – son of Shelemiah, son of Hananiah. Sentry at the Benjamin Gate who arrested Jeremiah on the charge of deserting to the Chaldeans (Jeremiah 37:12-14). May have been (and is assumed in this series to have been) grandson of the false prophet **Hananiah** [1], killed by God five years earlier (Jeremiah 28:15-17).

Ishmael – son of Nethaniah. Captain of an army unit in the open country and a member of the royal family (Jeremiah 41:1). One of the chief officers of King **Zedekiah** [1]. Went to **Gedaliah** [2] with other army leaders to seek assurances about the new regime after the destruction of Jerusalem and the kingdom of Judah. Appears to have been paid by Baalis the king of the Ammonites to kill Gedaliah [2], the newly appointed governor. Went with 10 men to Mizpah and assassinated Gedaliah [2], many of the Jews with him and all of the Chaldean soldiers who were there. Later killed some pilgrims as well. Took various people captive and set out for Ammon. He was chased by the other army commanders and overtaken at Gibeon. After some fighting, he escaped with eight men and went to the Ammonites (Jeremiah 41).

Ithmah – a Moabite diplomat who visited Jerusalem in the time of Jehoiakim. (Not in the Bible.)

Ishi – a servant of Immer. (Not in the Bible.)

Jaazaniah [1] – son of Jeremiah, son of Habazziniah. Descendant of Jonadab the son of Rechab and chief of the house of the Rechabites (Jeremiah 35:3). Jeremiah offered the Rechabites wine and they refused as commanded by Jonadab the son of Rechab (Jeremiah 35:6).

Jaazaniah [2] – son of Shaphan. Elder of Israel who led them in idolatry (seen by Ezekiel in a vision of events in Jerusalem (Ezekiel 8:11)).

Jaazaniah [3] – son of Azzur. Prince of the people who led them in worshipping the sun (seen by Ezekiel in a vision of events in Jerusalem (Ezekiel 11:1)). Possibly the brother of **Hananiah [1]** the false prophet (Jeremiah 28:1 and Ezekiel 11:1).

Jaazaniah [4] (also known as **Jezaniah**) – son of Hoshaiah the Maacathite. Captain of an army unit in the open country. Went to **Gedaliah [2]** with other army leaders to seek assurances about the new regime after the destruction of Jerusalem and the kingdom of Judah (2 Kings 25:23; Jeremiah 40:8; 42:1).

Jeconiah – son of King **Jehoiakim**. King of Judah for 3 months and 10 days after the death of his father. Also known as Coniah or Jehoiachin.

Jehiel – a chief officer of the temple in the time of King **Josiah** with **Hilkiah** and **Zechariah** (2 Chronicles 35:8).

Jehoahaz – see **Shallum [4]**.

Jehoiakim – son of King **Josiah**. King of Judah for 11 years after Pharaoh **Neco** deposed King **Jehoahaz (Shallum [4])**. Originally named Eliakim, but renamed by **Neco**.

Jehoiachin – see **Jeconiah**.

Jehonathan – one of King **Zedekiah**'s guards who was also a friend of **Ebed-melech** and helped him free **Jeremiah** from the cistern. (Not in the Bible.)

Jehozadak – son of **Seraiah [3]** (1 Chronicles 6:14) and great grandson of **Hilkiah** the High Priest. Taken into captivity by King **Nebuchadnezzar** (1 Chronicles 6:15) after his father was executed in Riblah. Assumed to be Jeremiah's great nephew. Probably brother of Ezra the priest, scribe and Bible author (Ezra 7:1-2).

Jehucal/Jucal – son of Shelemiah (Jeremiah 37:3 and 38:1). Official of King **Zedekiah**. With **Shepatiah**, **Gedaliah [1]** and **Pashhur [2]**, asked King **Zedekiah** to kill Jeremiah and then put Jeremiah into a mud-filled cistern (Jeremiah 38:1-6).

Jehudi – son of Nethaniah, son of **Shelemiah [1]**, son of Cushi (Jeremiah 36:14, 21 and 23). Sent by King **Jehoiakim**'s officials to fetch **Baruch** with the scroll he had written at Jeremiah's dictation. Read the scroll to King **Jehoiakim**, who cut it up and burned it (Jeremiah 36).

Jeiel – a leader of the Levites. Contributed offerings for the Levites in the great Passover ordered by King **Josiah** in the eighteenth year of his reign (2 Chronicles 35:9).

Jerahmeel – son of King **Jehoiakim** (or possibly of a man called Hammelech, which means "the king") (Jeremiah 36:26). Sent unsuccessfully with **Seraiah [1]** and **Shelemiah [2]** to arrest Jeremiah and **Baruch**.

Jeremiah – priest from Anathoth (Jeremiah 1:1). Son of Hilkiah, assumed to be **Hilkiah** the High Priest. Writer, under God's inspiration, of the book of Jeremiah.

Jezaniah – see **Jaazaniah [4]**.

Joah – son of Joahaz the recorder (2 Chronicles 34:8). Sent with **Shaphan** and **Maaseiah [1]** to supervise the repairing of the house of the Lord (2 Chronicles 34:8).

Johanan (and a brother Jonathan in some manuscripts) – the son(s) of Kareah. Captain(s) of an army unit in the open country. Went to **Gedaliah [2]** with other army leaders to seek assurances about the new regime after the destruction of Jerusalem and the kingdom of Judah. Warned **Gedaliah [2]**, the newly appointed governor, about a plot by Ishmael to kill him, but was ignored. Led the chase and fight against **Ishmael** after he had assassinated **Gedaliah [2]** and overtook them at Gibeon. Spokesmen for the people when asking Jeremiah to seek an answer from God as to whether the remnant should go to Egypt or not, and also led them in refusing to listen to God's answer. See Jeremiah 40, 42 and 43.

Jonathan – owner of a house turned into a prison during the siege of Jerusalem (Jeremiah 37:15-21; 38:28).

Josiah – son of **Amon** (2 Kings 21:24) and grandson of **Manasseh**, kings of Judah. Became king of Judah at the age of eight and reigned 31 years (2 Kings 22:1). Jeremiah began to prophesy in the thirteenth year of his reign (Jeremiah 1:2) and continued to prophesy throughout the rest of his reign (Jeremiah 25:3). He was named in a prophecy in 1 Kings 13:2 and his actions against idolatry in Israel predicted. He was the only king of Judah or Israel who had this name.

Jozabad – a leader of the Levites. Contributed offerings for the Levites in the great Passover ordered by King **Josiah** in the eighteenth year of his reign (2 Chronicles 35:9).

Kallai – a guard in the house of Jonathan when it was used as a prison. (Not in the Bible.)

Lappidoth – a captain of the king's guard who enjoyed telling stories of military events. Later led a group of soldiers fighting in the open country. (Not in the Bible.)

Maacah – daughter of **Miriam**, an inn-keeper in Bethel, and a believer in God. The inn was visited by Jeremiah during the reign of King **Josiah**. (Not in the Bible.)

Maaseiah [1] – governor of Jerusalem. Sent with **Shaphan** and **Joah** to supervise the repairing of the house of the Lord (2 Chronicles 34:8). May have been a priest and the father of **Zephaniah [2]** and **Zedekiah [2]**, but this is more likely to apply to **Maaseiah [2]**.

Maaseiah [2] – keeper of the threshold of the house of God (Jeremiah 35:4). May have been a priest and the father of **Zephaniah [2]** (second priest at the time of the destruction of Jerusalem (Jeremiah 37:3)) and/or **Zedekiah [2]** (a false prophet in exile (Jeremiah 29:25)).

Malchiah/Malchijah – son of King **Zedekiah [1]**, or possibly a man called Hammelech (which means "the king"). Owner of the cistern into which Jeremiah was put by **Shephatiah**, **Gedaliah [1]**, **Jehucal/Jucal** and **Pashhur [2]** (Jeremiah 38:1-6). Presumably killed by **Nebuchadnezzar** in Riblah with the other sons of King **Zedekiah** (Jeremiah 52:10).

Manasseh – son of King Hezekiah. Judah's worst king (2 Kings 23:26, 24:3). Began to reign at the age of 12 and reigned for 55 years. Repented near the end of his life, but the damage was done: Judah was sent into captivity because of Manasseh's evil (Jeremiah 15:4; see also 2 Kings 21:1-18 and 2 Chronicles 33:1-20).

Meshullam – a Levite of the family of Kohath. One of the overseers of the work of repairing and restoring the temple of God in the eighteenth year of King **Josiah** (2 Chronicles 34:12). Also worked as a Validator in Volume 2, but this is not in the Bible.

Micaiah – son of **Gemariah [2]**, son of **Shaphan** (Jeremiah 36:11). Told **Jehoiakim**'s officials of the words read by **Baruch** from the scroll dictated by Jeremiah (Jeremiah 36:11-13).

Micri – a noble of Judah during the reign of King **Josiah**. (Not in the Bible.)

Miriam – an inn-keeper in Bethel, and a believer in God. The inn was visited by Jeremiah during the reign of King **Josiah**. (Not in the Bible.)

Mishael – friend of **Daniel**, taken into captivity with him in the third/fourth year of King **Jehoiakim** (Daniel 1:1-2). In Babylon, his name was changed to Meshach (Daniel 1:6-7).

Mishael – the son of **Shobai** and **Maacah** in Bethel, taken into captivity in the third/fourth year of **King Jehoiakim**. (Not in the Bible).

Nathan – a young robber Jeremiah met while travelling in Israel. (Not in the Bible.)

Nebuchadnezzar – king of Babylon, mentioned in 2 Kings, 1 & 2 Chronicles, Ezra, Nehemiah, Esther, Jeremiah, Ezekiel and Daniel.

Nebushazban the Rab-saris (see also **Sar-sekim**). Senior official of Nebuchadnezzar the king of Babylon. One of a group of chief officials sent by Nebuchadnezzar to make sure Jeremiah was cared for after the fall of Jerusalem. (Jeremiah 39:13-14).

Nebuzaradan – captain of the guard for **Nebuchadnezzar**, king of Babylon (2 Kings 25:8). Freed Jeremiah from among the prisoners being taken to Babylon (Jeremiah 40:1) and left him with **Gedaliah [2]**. Burned the temple and the king's house, destroyed all important buildings in the city and broke down the walls (2 Kings 25:8-10). Took many Jews into captivity in Babylon, leaving only a few of the poorest people in the land (2 Kings 25:11-12). Took away the bronze and the vessels of the temple (2 Kings 25:13-17). Took many officials to King **Nebuchadnezzar** in Riblah where they were executed (2 Kings 25:18-21). Also took more Jews captive 4-5 years later (Jeremiah 52:30).

Pharaoh **Neco** – king of Egypt in the time of **Josiah** (2 Kings 23:29). Marched through Judah on the way to Carchemish to help Assyria fight with **Nebuchadnezzar** at the command of God (2 Chronicles 35:20-22). Met **Josiah** in battle and killed him (2 Chronicles 35:23-24). Deposed **Jehoahaz** on the way back three months later (2 Chronicles 36:1-4). Fought in the battle of Carchemish four years later and lost (Jeremiah 46:2). This was the end of Egypt's power over other kingdoms.

Nehushta – daughter of Elnathan of Jerusalem. Wife of King **Jehoiakim** and mother of King **Jeconiah** (2 Kings 24:6, 8).

Nergal-sar-ezer [1] – official of **Nebuchadnezzar** the king of Babylon. Met with other Chaldean officials in the middle gate of Jerusalem after a breach was opened in the wall (Jeremiah 39:3).

Nergal-sar-ezer [2] – the Rab-mag. Official of **Nebuchadnezzar** the king of Babylon. Met with other Chaldean officials in the middle gate of Jerusalem after a breach was opened in the wall (Jeremiah 39:3). One of a group of chief officials sent by **Nebuchadnezzar** to make sure Jeremiah was cared for after the fall of Jerusalem (Jeremiah 39:13).

Nethanel – a leader of the Levites with his brothers **Shemaiah** [3] and **Conaniah**. Contributed offerings for the Levites in the great Passover ordered by King **Josiah** in the eighteenth year of his reign (2 Chronicles 35:9).

Omri – senior officer of the king's guard. (Not in the Bible.)

Ozem – leader of a squad of soldiers protecting King **Jehoiakim** when the Chaldean army attacked in his eleventh year. (Not in the Bible.)

Pashhur [1] – son of Immer. A priest, chief officer of the temple. Assaulted Jeremiah and then imprisoned him in the stocks for a day. Cursed by God (Jeremiah 20:1-6).

Pashhur [2] – son of Malchiah. One of King Zedekiah's nobles. Sent by King **Zedekiah** [1] to ask for God's advice when King **Nebuchadnezzar** was besieging Jerusalem (Jeremiah 21:1-7). With **Shephatiah**, **Gedaliah** [1] and **Jehucal/Jucal**, later asked King Zedekiah [1] to kill Jeremiah and then put Jeremiah in the mud-filled cistern (Jeremiah 38:1-6). Father of Jeroham, whose son Adaiah returned from captivity (1 Chronicles 9:12).

Pelatiah – son of **Benaiah** [2]. Prince of the people who led them in worshipping the sun (Ezekiel 8:16; 11:1). Died in one of Ezekiel's visions of events in Jerusalem (Ezekiel 11:13).

Ram – one of the soldiers of **Ishmael**, the son of Nethaniah. Carried a message to **Johanan**. (Not in the Bible.)

Rei – a servant in the house of **Azariah** [1] when he was High Priest. (Not in the Bible.)

Samgar-nebu – official of **Nebuchadnezzar** the king of Babylon. Met with other Chaldean officials in the middle gate of Jerusalem after a breach was opened in the wall (Jeremiah 39:3).

Sar-sekim – the Rab-saris (see also **Nebushazban**). Official of **Nebuchadnezzar** the king of Babylon. Met with other Chaldean officials in the middle gate of Jerusalem after a breach was opened in the wall (Jeremiah 39:3).

Seraiah [1] – son of Azriel. A servant of King **Jehoiakim** sent unsuccessfully to arrest Jeremiah and **Baruch** (Jeremiah 36:26).

Seraiah [2] – son of Neriah, son of Mahseiah (Jeremiah 51:59). Quartermaster who went with King **Zedekiah** to Babylon (Jeremiah 51:59). Jeremiah sent a message with him on a scroll (Jeremiah 51:59-64). Brother of **Baruch** (Jeremiah 32:12; 51:59).

Seraiah [3] – Grandson of **Hilkiah** the High Priest (1 Chronicles 6:13 and Ezra 7:1). High Priest after **Azariah** [1], the son of **Hilkiah**. High Priest at the time of the destruction of Jerusalem, killed by **Nebuchadnezzar** (2 Kings 25:18-21). Father of **Jehozadak** who was taken into exile. Assumed to be the nephew of Jeremiah.

Seraiah [4] – son of Tanhumeth the Netophathite. A captain of the army of Judah at the time of the destruction of Jerusalem (2 Kings 25:23 and Jeremiah 40:8). Went to **Gedaliah** [2] with other army leaders to seek assurances about the new regime after the destruction of Jerusalem and the kingdom of Judah.

Shallum [1] – High Priest and father of **Hilkiah** the High Priest (1 Chronicles 6:13). Assumed to be Jeremiah's grandfather.

Shallum [2] – Jeremiah's uncle (Jeremiah 32:7). Assumed to be the brother of **Hilkiah** the High Priest.

Shallum [3] – Keeper of the wardrobe and husband of **Huldah** the prophetess (2 Chronicles 34:22). Described as son of Tikvah, son of Harhas in 2 Kings 22:14 or son of Tokhath, son of Hasrah in 2 Chronicles 34:22.

Shallum [4] – Another name for **Jehoahaz** the son of **Josiah**. King of Judah for three months after the death of King **Josiah**. Deposed by Pharaoh **Neco** on his way back from Carchemish and imprisoned in Egypt until his death (Jeremiah 22:11-12 and 2 Kings 23:30-34, 2 Chronicles 36:1-4).

Shaphan – son of Azaliah, son of Meshullam (2 Kings 22:3). Secretary to King **Josiah**. Sent with **Maaseiah [1]** and **Joah** to supervise the repairing of the house of the Lord (2 Chronicles 34:8). Showed and read the book of the law to **Josiah** after it was found by **Hilkiah**. Sent with **Hilkiah**, **Achbor**, **Ahikam** (probably his son) and **Asaiah** to see **Huldah** the prophetess (2 Kings 22:11-20). Probably father of **Ahikam** and **Elasah** (Jeremiah 29:1-3).

Shelemiah [1] – son of Cushi. Father of Nethaniah whose son **Jehudi** was sent by officials to fetch the scroll written by **Baruch** (Jeremiah 36:14).

Shelemiah [2] – son of Abdeel. A servant of King **Jehoiakim**, sent unsuccessfully to arrest Jeremiah and **Baruch** (Jeremiah 36:26).

Shemaiah [1] – a leader among the Levites in King **Josiah**'s time (2 Chronicles 35:9). Possibly the father of **Delaiah [1]** (Jeremiah 36:12).

Shemaiah [2] – the Nehelamite. False prophet in captivity in Babylon (Jeremiah 29:24-32). Sent unauthorised and rebellious letters to Jerusalem (Jeremiah 29:32).

Shemaiah [3] – a leader of the Levites with his brothers **Conaniah** and **Nethanel**. Contributed offerings for the Levites in the great Passover ordered by King **Josiah** in the eighteenth year of his reign (2 Chronicles 35:9).

Shephatiah – son of Mattan. Official of King **Zedekiah [1]**. With **Gedaliah [1]**, **Jehucal/Jucal** and **Pashhur [2]**, asked King **Zedekiah [1]** to kill Jeremiah, then put Jeremiah in a cistern partly filled with mud (Jeremiah 38:1-6).

Shobai – inhabitant of Bethel, and a believer in God. First met Jeremiah during the reign of King **Josiah**. (Not in the Bible.)

Telah – Captain of the guard at the Benjamin Gate during the reign of **Jeconiah**. (Not in the Bible.)

Uriah – son of Shemaiah from Kiriath-jearim. Prophet killed on the orders of King **Jehoiakim** for prophesying against Jerusalem (Jeremiah 26:20-23).

Vaniah – a guard in the house of Jonathan when it was used as a prison. (Not in the Bible.)

Zaccai – husband of **Abigail** [2]. Official/ruler/noble in the time of King **Josiah**. Welcomed visitors at the Passover in **Josiah**'s eighteenth year. (Not in the Bible.)

Zadok – son of **Azariah** [1], Jeremiah's brother. (Not in the Bible.)

Zebidah – daughter of Pedaiah of Rumah and wife of King **Josiah**. Mother of **Jehoiakim** (2 Kings 23:36).

Zechariah – a chief officer of the temple in the time of King **Josiah** with **Hilkiah** and **Jehiel** (2 Chronicles 35:8).

Zedekiah [1] – son of **Josiah**, king of Judah, and **Hamutal** the daughter of Jeremiah of Libnah (Jeremiah 52:1). Originally known as Mattaniah but renamed by King **Nebuchadnezzar** (2 Kings 24:17).

Zedekiah [2] – son of Maaseiah (possibly **Maaseiah [2]**). False prophet (with **Ahab** the son of Kolaiah) in captivity. Cursed by God in a letter sent by Jeremiah, with the punishment being that King **Nebuchadnezzar** would roast them in the fire (Jeremiah 29:21-23).

Zedekiah [3] – son of **Hananiah [2]** (Jeremiah 36:12). An official of King **Jehoiakim**.

Zephaniah [1] – son of Cushi, son of Gedaliah, son of Amariah, son of Hezekiah (probably King Hezekiah) (Zephaniah 1:1). Author, under the inspiration of God, of the book of Zephaniah.

Zephaniah [2] – son of Maaseiah (possibly **Maaseiah [2]**). A priest. Messenger sent to Jeremiah by King **Zedekiah [1]** near the end of his reign (Jeremiah 21:1-7; 29:24-29; 37:3-10). Probably executed by King **Nebuchadnezzar** (Jeremiah 52:24-27).

Zimri – a robber Jeremiah met while travelling in Israel. (Not in the Bible.)

Free Download

Paul in Snippets

A 109-page PDF novelette by Mark Morgan.

The life of Paul painted from the Acts of the Apostles.

Get your free copy of *Paul in Snippets* when you sign up for the Bible Tales mailing list. As well as the eBook, you will receive a weekly email newsletter with micro tales, informative articles and special offers.

Visit **https://www.BibleTales.online/free-pins**

Bible Tales Online

Other books by Mark Morgan are available from Bible Tales Online including other books in this series.

Terror on Every Side!

The Life of Jeremiah

From a family of priests in the peaceful reign of good King Josiah, came a young man Jeremiah, bringing words from God to his people. It was no message for the fainthearted, either. It was a message of *Terror on Every Side!*

Volume 1 – Early Days
Volume 2 – As Good As It Gets
Volume 3 – Darkness Falling
Volume 4 – The Darkness Deepens
Volume 5 – No Remedy

Generally available as paperback, eBook and audiobook.

To find the list of currently available books, visit

https://www.BibleTales.online/books

9 781925 587098

Josiah's family tree

When Jeremiah began to prophecy, Josiah was in the thirteenth year of his reign as king of Judah. At that time, he was 21 years old, having begun to reign when he was only eight years old.

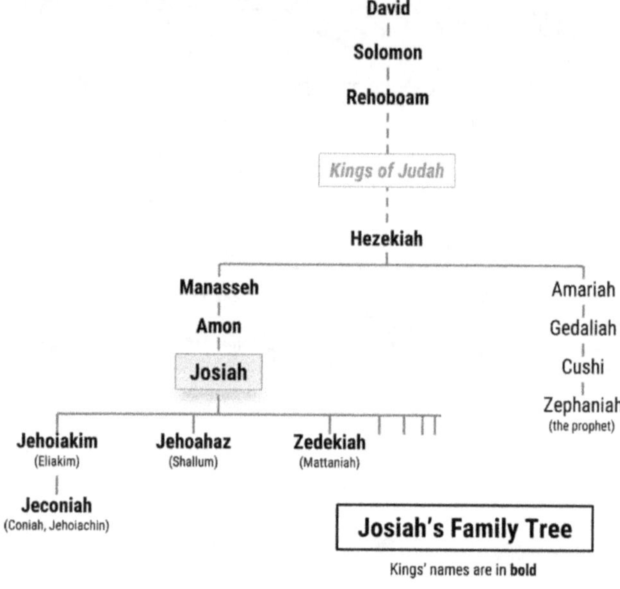

Josiah's Family Tree

Kings' names are in **bold**